Agatha Christie®

A Murder is Announced

Leslie Darbon

adapted from a story by
Agatha Christie

A SAMUEL FRENCH ACTING EDITION

SAMUEL FRENCH

FOUNDED 1830

SAMUELFRENCH.COM
SAMUELFRENCH-LONDON.CO.UK

ISBN 978-0-573-70245-7

www.SamuelFrench.com
www.SamuelFrench-London.co.uk

FOR PRODUCTION ENQUIRIES

UNITED STATES AND CANADA
Info@SamuelFrench.com
1-866-598-8449

UNITED KINGDOM AND EUROPE
Theatre@SamuelFrench-London.co.uk
020-7255-4302

Each title is subject to availability from Samuel French, depending upon country of performance. Please be aware that *A MURDER IS ANNOUNCED* may not be licensed by Samuel French in your territory. Professional and amateur producers should contact the nearest Samuel French office or licensing partner to verify availability.

MUSIC USE NOTE

Licensees are solely responsible for obtaining formal written permission from copyright owners to use copyrighted music in the performance of this play and are strongly cautioned to do so. If no such permission is obtained by the licensee, then the licensee must use only original music that the licensee owns and controls. Licensees are solely responsible and liable for all music clearances and shall indemnify the copyright owners of the play(s) and their licensing agent, Samuel French, against any costs, expenses, losses and liabilities arising from the use of music by licensees. Please contact the appropriate music licensing authority in your territory for the rights to any incidental music.

IMPORTANT BILLING AND CREDIT REQUIREMENTS

If you have obtained performance rights to this title, please refer to your licensing agreement for important billing and credit requirements.

A MURDER IS ANNOUNCED was first produced by by Peter Saunders at the Theatre Royal in Brighton, and subsequently at the Vaudeville Theatre in London, on September 21st, 1977. The performance was directed by Robert Chetwyn, with sets by Anthony Holland. The cast was as follows:

JULIA SIMMONS	Patricia Brake
LETITIA BLACKLOCK	Dinah Sheridan
DORA BUNNER	Eleanor Summerfield
PATRICK SIMMONS	Christopher Scoular
MITZI	Mia Nadasi
MISS MARPLE	Dulcie Gray
PHILLIPA HAYMES	Barbara Flynn
MRS SWETTENHAM	Nancy Nevinson
EDMUND SWETTENHAM	Gareth Armstrong
RUDI SCHERZ	Michael Dyerball
INSPECTOR CRADDOCK	James Grout
SERGEANT MELLORS	Michael Fleming

CHARACTERS

JULIA SIMMONS

LETITIA BLACKLOCK

DORA BUNNER

PATRICK SIMMONS

MITZI

MISS MARPLE

PHILLIPA HAYMES

MRS SWETTENHAM

EDMUND SWETTENHAM

RUDI SCHERZ

INSPECTOR CRADDOCK

SERGEANT MELLORS

SETTING

The action takes place in two drawing-rooms in an early Victorian house in Chipping Cleghorn which have been made into one room

ACT ONE
Scene I: The morning of Friday the 13th
Scene II: 6.10 p.m. the same day
Scene III: The following Saturday morning

ACT TWO
Scene I: The following Sunday afternoon
Scene II: The following Monday morning
Scene III: 6 p.m. the same day

TIME

Agatha Christie time

ACT ONE

Scene I

(Two drawing-rooms in an early Victorian house in Chipping Cleghorn which have been made into one room. The morning of Friday the thirteenth. The wall which originally separated the two rooms was clearly a bearer-wall since part of it has had to be left intact. This is upstage and has a door almost directly next to it. This door is kept locked and will be referred to as the Locked Door. In front of the remaining piece of wall – which juts out into the room – there is an occasional table of some quality. It is a real craftsman's piece with fine cabriole legs, beautifully carved. It is placed in this position in an attempt to help "integrate" the two rooms more. On this table there is a Dresden lamp. A shepherdess. A quality piece of porcelain. Beside it is a silver cigarette-box which is kept highly polished. Beside the "jutting out" piece of wall left, is a Sheraton bureau – without doubt a delight to live with. On top of this is an exquisite Art Nouveau china vase. Something very distinctive. Further along left, we come to the Main Door. A very wide door since it was fashioned in the days when ladies wore crinolines and the width made it easier for them to pass through into the room. In the left wall is a large fireplace with a carved surround – well in keeping with the general surroundings. On the mantelpiece we find a magnificent clock. French in origin – Empire period – of a predominantly squarish shape but with beautiful ornamental brasswork. It has the most exquisite chime. To one side of the fireplace there is a sideboard which

7

contains drinks and glasses, etc. It is heavy and not quite the same taste as the other pieces of furniture – but, it is practical.)

(In what was the smaller of the two drawing-rooms, right, there is a bay window. It reaches from floor to ceiling as was the custom in all houses during the period this one was built. It has rich velvet and net curtains. In the bay is a sofa. The walls are festooned with paintings. Not especially good, since most of them are family portraits. There are also a few late eighteenth- early nineteenth- century silhouettes, which were done when the family were not so well off as they had been. In a further attempt to disguise the fact that it was originally two rooms, the chairs are set in a semicircle. Most people will not be conscious of this and, of course, this is what was hoped for. There are quite a few interesting and comfortable chairs. Two spoon-backs. One grandmother and one grandfather. An upright "throne" chair. A low tub-shape. A fat comfortable looking button-back; and so on. In the middle of the cleverly placed semicircle there is a small centre table of good shape and nicely proportioned. It is not a big table and can easily be lifted by one person. There is a central light – probably a chandelier – and some wall lights.)

(The whole effect is of simple elegance. Not something merely to look at although pleasing to the eye – it is something to be lived in.)

*(As the curtain rises, **MISS BLACKLOCK** is at the bay window waving good-bye to someone. She is beyond middle-age, but still a very attractive woman who has clearly looked after her figure and features. **JULIA SIMMONS**, her niece, aged twenty-five or twenty-six, is sitting in a chair reading a newspaper.)*

MISS BLACKLOCK. Good-bye.

JULIA. You really do make too much fuss of her, Aunt Letty...

(**MISS BLACKLOCK** *turns from the window and moves to* **JULIA** *– a small smile on her face.*)

MISS BLACKLOCK. Well, Phillipa's been through rather a lot, Julia. And tell me what's wrong with trying to make life a bit more pleasant?

JULIA. Nothing – I suppose…

MISS BLACKLOCK. It's such a little thing – waving good-bye. But, it helps. I'd do the same for you.

JULIA. I'm family!

(**MISS BLACKLOCK** *picks up a newspaper and sits in a chair.*)

MISS BLACKLOCK. *(chuckling)* Why, Julia. It sounds as if you're jealous.

JULIA. Me? Certainly not! But, she is only a lodger.

MISS BLACKLOCK. Come to that. So are you.

(*A moment passes.* **JULIA** *appears a little hurt.*)

Look. I was pleased to have you here – and just as pleased to have Phillipa. She's had a lot to contend with. How would you feel if your husband had died so young leaving you with a child…

JULIA. I don't know. *I* wouldn't have got married in my teens. I'm not so daft.

MISS BLACKLOCK. Ah – the trouble is, we're not all as worldly as you are, Julia.

(*a moment's pause as* **MISS BLACKLOCK***'s point registers*)

JULIA. I'm sorry, Aunt Letty…

MISS BLACKLOCK. Oh – there's no need…

JULIA. No, no – I've been spiteful. And, believe it or not, I rather like Phillipa. We seem to be on the same wave length. But, you do make too much fuss – of all of us.

MISS BLACKLOCK. I like having young people around me. So when your mother asked if you could stay here, I was delighted. It meant I could indulge myself…

(*The Main Door opens and* **DORA BUNNER** *enters. She is slightly older than* **MISS BLACKLOCK**.)

BUNNY. I can't find it, Letty. I can't find it *anywhere.*

(**MISS BLACKLOCK** *looks up from her newspaper and smiles benignly.*)

MISS BLACKLOCK. What dear?

(**BUNNY** *goes to her.*)

BUNNY. It's Friday…

MISS BLACKLOCK. (*with a wry smile*) All day, dear.

BUNNY. Yes.

JULIA. Friday, the thirteenth to be precise. *Ominous!*

BUNNY. (*worried*) Oh, dear… What was I saying, Letty?

MISS BLACKLOCK. You couldn't find *it,* Bunny dear.

BUNNY. Exactly. I can't find it anywhere. Have you seen it?

MISS BLACKLOCK. (*smiling*) Let's start at the beginning.

BUNNY. It's Friday – I always read it Friday morning after breakfast…

MISS BLACKLOCK. Oh, the *Gazette,* you mean…

BUNNY. Of course. That's what I've been telling you…

MISS BLACKLOCK. Yes, dear…

BUNNY. I can't find the *Chipping Cleghorn Gazette* anywhere. (*with a sudden thought*) You don't think they've gone on strike, do you?

MISS BLACKLOCK. They wouldn't do that, dear. Not *here.*

JULIA. What a lovely thought. A strike. Here. *Picket lines –* headlines in the national press… We might even be on the wireless. "Reporters on *Chipping Cleghorn Gazette* refuse to report Vicar's garden party."

MISS BLACKLOCK. Things like that don't happen here…

JULIA. No. *Nothing* happens here. It's another world, isn't it?

MISS BLACKLOCK. And just as well, too.

(PATRICK SIMMONS, JULIA's brother enters through the Main Door, reading the Chipping Cleghorn Gazette. He is a year older than his sister; a very handsome young man. He chuckles as he reads.)

PATRICK. Listen to this. It's marvellous. Abso-blooming-lutely marvellous.

JULIA. *(sarcastically)* Oh, Patrick – *do* tell us what it is. We're all dying to know.

PATRICK. Oh, dear. We are in a bad mood, aren't we? Have a bad dream last night?

JULIA. A nightmare. It was all about you.

PATRICK. Well – it's better than being ignored…

MISS BLACKLOCK. What's so marvellous, Patrick?

PATRICK. The Personal Column in this rag, Aunt Letty. It's better than Evelyn Home. Listen to this. *(reading)* "Young woman, said to be excitingly beautiful, seeks companionship with mature man. Love. Marriage. Rolls-Royce owners only." *(He looks at* **BUNNY.**) Really, Bunny. I'm surprised at you. Wouldn't a Bentley owner be just as suitable?

MISS BLACKLOCK. *(to* **PATRICK**) You know very well, young man, that Bunny *always* reads the *Gazette* first. I don't have many rules in this house but that's one. She's been looking everywhere for it.

PATRICK. Well – she could have borrowed Mitzi's.

JULIA. Mitzi?

PATRICK. She thinks it will help her to speak English.

*(**BUNNY** comes back to life again at the mention of* **MITZI.**)

BUNNY. Oh, dear me, no. I couldn't – I really couldn't. I've only got to walk past the kitchen and she snarls at me. I only want to help – that's all. I couldn't ask her – I just couldn't. She's horrid, that Millie.

MISS BLACKLOCK. Mitzi, dear.

BUNNY. Yes.

MISS BLACKLOCK. Well, you won't have to ask her, Bunny.

PATRICK. It's all yours, Bunny. *(He gives her the newspaper.)*

BUNNY. Thank you, Patrick.

PATRICK. And I promise I won't borrow it again.

BUNNY. *(coldly)* Why aren't you at College? It wouldn't have happened if you'd been at College…

PATRICK. I haven't got a lecture till this afternoon.

BUNNY. All that grant you get – and you never seem to do anything.

PATRICK. It's not my fault.

MISS BLACKLOCK. Just enjoy your paper, Bunny…

> *(**MISS BLACKLOCK** gently pats **BUNNY**'s shoulder. **BUNNY** opens the Gazette and starts reading.)*

You *are* very lucky, Patrick…

PATRICK. I'm quite willing to go to more lectures.

JULIA. It's one giant holiday for him.

PATRICK. Oh, thanks for nothing – *sister!* Anyway listen to who's talking about a holiday – you've got the *whole* day off.

JULIA. Only because I've worked over-time – *every* night this week.

PATRICK. Huh! Pull the other one. I wouldn't be surprised if you haven't been working over-time at all. Been to the *pictures* more likely.

> *(There is an odd glare between them. They hold it a moment.)*

MISS BLACKLOCK. My goodness, you two – did you always bicker like this at home?

JULIA. *He* did. *I* didn't!

> *(Quite suddenly **BUNNY** sits upright.)*

BUNNY. Letty! Letty!

> *(**BUNNY**'s tone is enough to make **MISS BLACKLOCK** get to her feet.)*

MISS BLACKLOCK. What is it, Bunny? What's wrong?

BUNNY. Letty, dear. What does it mean?

(MISS BLACKLOCK moves to BUNNY.)

Oh, my goodness. Whatever can it mean?

MISS BLACKLOCK. I won't know unless you tell me.

(BUNNY indicates the newspaper.)

BUNNY. Here. In the *Gazette*. Right at the bottom of the Personal Column.

MISS BLACKLOCK. Yes, dear?

BUNNY. It's an announcement...

MISS BLACKLOCK. How nice.

BUNNY. No, no – you don't understand...

MISS BLACKLOCK. No, I know I don't.

BUNNY. It says... Oh, dear – I can't bear to read it...

JULIA. *(sweetly)* But, you will...

(BUNNY glares at JULIA.)

BUNNY. Yes. *(Reading)* "A murder is announced and will take place on Friday, October the thirteenth, at Little Paddocks – at six-thirty P.M. Friends please accept this, the only intimation."

(BUNNY looks up at MISS BLACKLOCK.)

MISS BLACKLOCK. Are you sure that's what it says?

(BUNNY indicates the newspaper.)

BUNNY. Right at the bottom...

MISS BLACKLOCK. This house? Little Paddocks?

BUNNY. Yes.

PATRICK. Read it again, Bunny.

BUNNY. *(reading)* "A murder is announced and will take place on Friday October the thirteenth...

JULIA. *(interrupting)* Today! I knew something dreadful was going to happen.

MISS BLACKLOCK. A few minutes ago you were complaining that *nothing* happened here. *(to BUNNY)* Finish it.

BUNNY. *(reading)* "… at Little Paddocks at six-thirty P.M. Friends please accept this, the only intimation."

(BUNNY stops reading and looks around at them. It's an awkward moment as they look from one to the other)

Oh, Letty…

MISS BLACKLOCK. Let me see. *(She takes the newspaper from BUNNY.)* JULIA. It's a joke.

(MISS BLACKLOCK looks up at her.)

Well, it has to be. I mean, who'd be daft enough to advertise a *real* murder in the newspapers.

PATRICK. A madman might…

MISS BLACKLOCK. It's nothing to do with you, is it, Patrick?

PATRICK. I'm not potty.

JULIA. That's debatable.

PATRICK. Ho ho!

MISS BLACKLOCK. *(turning to JULIA)* I wouldn't put it past you.

(JULIA is quickly on the defensive – perhaps a little too quickly.)

JULIA. It's nothing to do with me. Perhaps Phillipa can throw some light on it.

PATRICK. No, it's not the sort of thing she'd get up to, anyway.

MISS BLACKLOCK. I agree! Well *someone* seems to think it's amusing.

BUNNY. It frightens me.

MISS BLACKLOCK. It's nothing to worry about.

BUNNY. But what will happen at six-thirty?

PATRICK. Delicious Death!

BUNNY. *(hand to mouth)* Oh…

MISS BLACKLOCK. *Really*, Patrick!

JULIA. He means Mitzi's special cake. We always call it Delicious Death.

PATRICK. Yes Bunny. *(reading)* "Friends, please accept this, the only intimation." Somebody's bound to drop round. I thought we might get her to make one.

MISS BLACKLOCK. I'm sure you did. *(to BUNNY)* Nothing will happen at six-thirty, Bunny. Except Patrick is probably right in suggesting that one or two people might drop in out of curiosity.

JULIA. It might turn into a party.

MISS BLACKLOCK. It most certainly won't!

PATRICK. *(trying to make amends)* So, there's nothing to worry about, Bunny. Nothing.

BUNNY. *You really think so?*

PATRICK. Of course.

BUNNY. Oh, good. That makes me feel better.

MISS BLACKLOCK. We'll all laugh about it tomorrow, Bunny.

BUNNY. Yes. *(She starts to read again. The crisis is over.)*

(There is a moment's pause, then the Main Door opens and MITZI, MISS BLACKLOCK's cook, enters, brandishing a copy of the Gazette. She is about twenty-five or twenty-six, small and dark – a mid-European, (Hungary, Roumania or perhaps Yugoslavia). She is an explosive character inclined to believe that everyone is against her. At the moment she is in one of her moods – upset and crackling.)

MITZI. Someone is after me. I am going to be murdered in my bed!

(BUNNY is immediately alert to the tension.)

BUNNY. Murdered!

MITZI. It is here. In the *Gazette.* They are coming for me.

MISS BLACKLOCK. Whoever put that silly advert in the paper obviously did it with the precise intention of sending this house into total chaos!

MITZI. There will be blood everywhere. They will cut me up and feed me to the dogs.

PATRICK. Poor dogs!

(MITZI turns to him.)

MITZI. It will happen. In this very house. If I stay! *Tonight!* *(She waves the newspaper under his nose.)* It is here – in this newspaper. They come to get me. At six-thirty tonight! You see – they care nothing for the law. They tell everyone they are coming to *murder* me... *(She goes into Hungarian.) Örulet örulet nire Kepesek...*

(MITZI turns to leave, but MISS BLACKLOCK stops her.)

MISS BLACKLOCK. No one's going to murder you. It's a joke.

MITZI. I not laugh. I go!

MISS BLACKLOCK. Nevertheless, I don't think it has anything to do with you.

MITZI. You don't know. Once you have escaped – they never let you get away...

BUNNY. But I thought you did get away...

MITZI. They hound me. Day and night. Night and day. The telephone calls. You wonder what they are – who they are from...

JULIA. What telephone calls?

MITZI. Agents. From my country. Why? Why do you think they keep phoning me?

BUNNY. I expect they want to know how you're getting on over here, Millie.

MISS BLACKLOCK. But, Mitzi, I've never heard you get a telephone call.

MITZI. They do it in secret. They never leave me alone. They don't like it that I escape from them. Oh! You have no idea what it is like. They interrogate me. For days – weeks – months. The light shining in my eyes. My family – they send them to Siberia. *(She continues in Hungarian.) De èn nem török meg! Nem mondom meg amit tudok. Tuljàrok az eszukön es elszököm a szabad földre. Most jönnek utanam de en megyek!*

MISS BLACKLOCK. Mitzi! Do be sensible about this. Nothing is going to happen to you. No one is going to come after you. No spy. No agent. So calm yourself down – we'll all look after you. Now. This is what I suggest you do. You get that beef out of the pantry and make that special goulash of yours for lunch.

(There is a sudden and dramatic change in MITZI's attitude.)

MITZI. Oh! You like my goulash – eh?

MISS BLACKLOCK. It's simply delicious.

MITZI. I make it even more special for you today. I put in some wine – some rich, red wine from Hungary... *(She kisses her fingers to express her feelings about the goulash.)* It makes my mouth water just to think of it!

MISS BLACKLOCK. Good. You do that. Incidentally, I expect someone or other might be dropping in around six-thirty this evening.

(But, even as she says this, MISS BLACKLOCK regrets it. MITZI immediately reacts.)

MITZI. To murder me!

MISS BLACKLOCK. *(irritatedly)* No, no, no!

MITZI. Why they come?

(MISS BLACKLOCK places a reassuring hand on MITZI's shoulder.)

MISS BLACKLOCK. For a drink – and a sandwich perhaps. And you make such good sandwiches.

MITZI. *(still suspicious)* It will be all right?

MISS BLACKLOCK. There's nothing to worry about...

(A moment, as MITZI considers.)

MITZI. You are right. I am a good cook, no? I make a dip, too.

MISS BLACKLOCK. Well – yes. But not too much garlic, please.

MITZI. You not like garlic?

MISS BLACKLOCK. Well, yes – in moderation. But, after the last dip you made we were totally isolated in Church on Sunday – and that was two days after we'd eaten it!

MITZI. I tell you then. I use only two cloves of garlic this time – instead of my usual seven. But it not be nearly so good. I go now. Too long you have kept me gas-bagging.

(With this **MITZI** *turns and exits quickly.)*

*(***PATRICK*** claps his hands, applauding.)*

PATRICK. Well done, Aunt Letty.

JULIA. Yes, beautifully handled.

MISS BLACKLOCK. How nice to have you two in agreement for once.

BUNNY. Letty was always very good with people. She could have gone a long way. Yes, a long way indeed – if only –

*(***MISS BLACKLOCK*** cuts across her quickly and we might spot just a slight meaningful glance.)*

MISS BLACKLOCK. Now, now, Bunny dear. We mustn't keep reminiscing. Young people aren't interested in the past these days.

*(***BUNNY*** gets the message.)*

BUNNY. *(flustered)* Dear me – I am so silly. I get so muddled lately. I am sorry, Letty. Really and truly sorry.

MISS BLACKLOCK. Bunny – I wasn't angry with you.

BUNNY. But, you're so right – everything's mixed up – I must be more careful – and think before I say something…

MISS BLACKLOCK. No one minds – we all understand. Read your paper, dear – you know how much you enjoy it.

BUNNY. Yes. That's what I'll do. But, I won't read that advertisement again, Letty.

MISS BLACKLOCK. *(a little despairingly)* No, dear – don't do that.

BUNNY. I shan't sleep a wink tonight though Mitzi could be right. We might all be murdered in our beds.

MISS BLACKLOCK. *(biting back the irritation)* No, dear, no. The advertisement says six-thirty. I don't think any of us will be in our beds by then.

BUNNY. *(after a moment)* Oh, no. We won't, will we?

MISS BLACKLOCK. So, there's nothing to worry about.

(BUNNY goes back to her paper, but, just as quickly, she puts it back down again.)

BUNNY. We could be murdered down here just as easily as upstairs!

MISS BLACKLOCK. Bunny!

BUNNY. Oh, no, don't do that Letty, please.

MISS BLACKLOCK. *(relenting)* Well, then.

(BUNNY goes back to the paper and stays reading it this time.)

JULIA. For a moment there I could see Mitzi clearing off and me having to do the cooking from now on... *(She turns sharply to PATRICK.)* And you needn't make any comment – thank you very much!

PATRICK. I was just thinking what a terrible liar Mitzi is.

JULIA. We all know she doesn't get any phone calls.

PATRICK. And what about her parents being sent to Siberia. Last time she told us they were executed in Red Square...

JULIA. While she stood there in the snow, with tears freezing on her cheeks.

MISS BLACKLOCK. We must be sympathetic towards her. She's lonely. Life must be pretty miserable with no-one you can talk to – no one from your background. I suppose that's why she makes up all these stories.

PATRICK. Lies, you mean!

MISS BLACKLOCK. Yes, I do, But I think I can see why she does it.

JULIA. Why are her stories always such doom, gloom and disaster.

MISS BLACKLOCK. That's what she enjoys. Like some people enjoy reading murder mysteries.

(*There is a knock on the Main Door. It opens, and* **MISS MARPLE** *enters, carrying a bunch of violets wrapped in tissue paper. She is an elderly lady with an over-inquisitive mind which gets her into all sorts of trouble*)

MISS MARPLE. The front door was open – I do hope I'm not intruding.

MISS BLACKLOCK. Not at all, Miss Marple…

(**MISS MARPLE** *moves into the room.*)

MISS MARPLE. Only I popped in to deliver these – (*She indicates the violets.*) – to Miss Bunny…

BUNNY. *beams brightly and gets to her feet*

BUNNY. Oh – oh, how lovely…

MISS MARPLE. You remember you admired them so at the Vicarage the other day. I told my nephew and he insisted I bring some along for you.

(*She hands them to* **BUNNY.**)

BUNNY. How kind. How very kind. (*She holds them out to* **MISS BLACKLOCK.**) Look, Letty. Aren't they lovely? And so unusual in the autumn.

MISS BLACKLOCK. My grandmother was able to grow them right up to the winter months. I adore violets.

MISS MARPLE. Yes, there's something very sentimental about them. Don't you think so, Julia?

JULIA. I think you have a very romantic nature, Miss Marple…

MISS MARPLE. Do you?

JULIA. But, I do see what you mean.

(**MISS MARPLE** *is close enough to* **PATRICK** *to give him a dig in the ribs.*)

MISS MARPLE. Well. I don't think Patrick does!

JULIA. There's no romance in *his* soul!

MISS MARPLE. Well, you're only his sister – you probably wouldn't see it if it was there.

BUNNY. Where shall they go, Letty? I want everyone to enjoy them.

MISS BLACKLOCK. What about here on the sideboard? There's even a vase waiting for them.

BUNNY. And it's already got water in it. It must be stale. I'll get some fresh. Won't be a minute.

(BUNNY *exits through Main Door with the violets and vase.*)

MISS BLACKLOCK. Do sit down. I'm so glad you called. I wanted to ask you to Bunny's birthday party on Sunday. I know she'd love you to be here.

MISS MARPLE. Thank you. I love parties. Perhaps there is something I can do to help.

JULIA. I'll be helping Aunt Letty, Miss Marple.

PATRICK. (*mimicking* JULIA) I'll be helping Aunt Letty, Miss Marple. Julia. Well, you'll be in bed till noon and you'll spend the rest of the day snoring in an armchair – so we can't rely on you for any help!

MISS MARPLE. The announcement in the *Gazette.* What does it mean?

MISS BLACKLOCK. You've seen that, have you?

MISS MARPLE. I should think everybody in Chipping Cleghorn has seen it by now. Has it anything to do with Miss Bunny's birthday?

JULIA. We've no idea what it means.

PATRICK. Probably some crank who thinks he's being funny.

MISS MARPLE. I see. I thought it was an invitation to play some sort of new game or something.

PATRICK. The murder game. Sounds good, doesn't it?

MISS BLACKLOCK. If you're interested Miss Marple, why don't you come along at six-thirty.

JULIA. Oh yes, do, Miss Marple.

MISS MARPLE. I'd love to but I have to go into Medenham Wells for my treatment and I'm not sure how long it's going to take. I'll do my best, though.

MISS BLACKLOCK. Is your rheumatism better?

MISS MARPLE. Very much, thank you. The spa waters are so good. Give it another week and I shall be back in St Mary Mead.

PATRICK. Chipping Cleghorn won't be the same without you!

MISS MARPLE. I shall miss it here. Although I think my niece won't be over sorry when I leave. They've been very patient with me.

JULIA. Would they like to come tonight?

MISS MARPLE. I'm sure they would love to. My nephew's very like me, he loves a mystery, but they're having dinner with the Bishop.

JULIA. It would have been rather reassuring to have the Vicar here.

MISS MARPLE. Knowing your neighbours, you won't be alone. The Colonel and Mrs. Easterbrook for a start...

PATRICK. No – they're in Bournemouth.

MISS MARPLE. Clara Swettenham wouldn't miss an opportunity like this. And young Edmund – with two beautiful young girls staying here.

JULIA. There's someone I could do without. And Phillipa says he's a layabout.

MISS MARPLE. I thought he was a writer.

JULIA. He is. But, she says it's an excuse not to get a real job and work for a living.

MISS MARPLE. *(smiling)* Perhaps she's got a point.

(**BUNNY** *enters with the violets in the vase.*)

BUNNY. Do thank the Vicar for me, Miss Marple. I'm touched – I really am. So kind of him.

MISS MARPLE. He was delighted you noticed them. He brought the original cutting back from Devon – the Dart Valley – he was born there.

BUNNY. *(distantly)* Devon violets. There's nothing quite like them. *(She crosses to the bureau and "arranges" them on top – trying a couple of different places before she is satisfied.)*

MISS MARPLE. Well, I must be going. I hope all will be well this evening.

(BUNNY looks across – she has forgotten.)

BUNNY. *(smiling)* What?

MISS MARPLE. The announcement – in the *Gazette*. A murder will take place here at six-thirty...

BUNNY. *(hand to mouth)* Oh – yes...

MISS MARPLE. If it wasn't a joke or some sort of game it would be very worrying for all of you.

MISS BLACKLOCK. We're made of sterner stuff than you think, Miss Marple.

MISS MARPLE. But, surely, Miss Blacklock. If there's going to be a murder there has to be a *victim*. If I were you the question I'd be asking myself is: who is going to be murdered?

(A moment. They look from one to the other. We see the first signs of real fear beginning to creep into their souls, as the curtain falls.)

Scene II

(The same. It is six-ten that evening.)

*(**MITZI** is putting things on the small centre table: glasses and drinks, sandwiches, the cheesy biscuits and the dip. **MISS BLACKLOCK** is filling the silver cigarette-box on the table by the jutting out wall.)*

MITZI. *(to **MISS BLACKLOCK**)* You like what I do, Miss Blacklock. Yes?

*(Having finished filling the cigarette box, **MISS BLACKLOCK** moves to **MITZI**.)*

MISS BLACKLOCK. Oh, yes – yes. Those do look nice, Mitzi. Thank you.

MITZI. The dip – well, it is not quite perfect. The sandwiches – in them I have put the pâté.

MISS BLACKLOCK. The pâté? Not my *pâté de fois gras?*

MITZI. It is delicious.

MISS BLACKLOCK. It was a present. It came from Fortnum's. I was saving that for a special occasion.

MITZI. You tell me to make sandwiches, I do it.

MISS BLACKLOCK. I was rather thinking of cheese.

MITZI. Huh! Your English cheese. It is like soap!

MISS BLACKLOCK. *We* like it.

MITZI. Do you need me anymore?

MISS BLACKLOCK. No, thank you, Mitzi. Are you going out?

MITZI. I have things to do in the dining-room. Then I go to my room and lock myself up.

MISS BLACKLOCK. *(smiling)* Before you go into hiding could you let the guests in when they arrive. I've decided to keep the front door locked this evening.

MITZI. *(explosively)* I am everything here. Head cook and bucket-washer.

MISS BLACKLOCK. Bottle-washer!

MITZI. Yes, that too!

(With this **MITZI** *turns smartly and exits through the Main Door, as* **JULIA** *enters.)*

JULIA. Not long now... Aren't you worried?

MISS BLACKLOCK. *(after a moment)* Why should I be?

JULIA. Well, supposing this isn't a hoax. Supposing some maniac is going to commit a murder here tonight?

MISS BLACKLOCK. You're the last person I expected to take it seriously. *(She turns on the main light.)*

JULIA. Well I do have a few butterflies in my stomach!

MISS BLACKLOCK. Well, have a drink and relax.

JULIA. What bothers me most is Miss Marple's comment.

MISS BLACKLOCK. Forget it. Miss Marple relishes this sort of thing. She's a real old busybody.

JULIA. But, quite a clever old busybody. And if she's right – who is going to be the victim?

MISS BLACKLOCK. *(impatiently)* No-one! Either it's a joke or it's someone who wants to get even. Someone I owe hospitality to and it's slipped my mind.

JULIA. But, if it isn't that –

MISS BLACKLOCK. *(irritatedly)* Julia...

JULIA. *(refusing to be stopped)* – One of us is going to die.

MISS BLACKLOCK. I *don't* want to hear any more – it's nonsense.

JULIA. It could be *you!* Or worse still *me!*

(MISS BLACKLOCK *draws the window curtains.)*

MISS BLACKLOCK. Oh, thank you very much.

JULIA. Well, it has to be someone in this house. Patrick – there are times when I could throttle him. Then there's Bunny.

MISS BLACKLOCK. Oh, perish the thought. Poor dear Bunny.

JULIA. I've seen you driven to distraction by her before now.

MISS BLACKLOCK. *(indignantly)* Yes, well… but we've been friends for years – from childhood. She can be irritating… What a horrible thought.

JULIA. Well on a happier note perhaps it will be Mitzi who gets the chop. She gets on my nerves.

MISS BLACKLOCK. That's not a good enough reason to murder her.

JULIA. Phillipa puzzles me. Who is she? Where does she come from?

MISS BLACKLOCK. You know exactly who she is – and where she comes from.

JULIA. We've only got her word for it.

MISS BLACKLOCK. The same applies to you and Patrick…

JULIA. But, Mother wrote to you – asked if we could stay here…

MISS BLACKLOCK. How do I know it wasn't a forgery?

JULIA. I see what you mean. But it wasn't.

MISS BLACKLOCK. I'm sure it wasn't. The same way I'm sure about Phillipa.

(**PATRICK** *enters by the Main Door, with* **PHILLIPA HAYMES**. *She is a tall, rather elegant-looking blonde of about twenty-six, with a touch of real class about her – a young lady with a rather serious turn of mind.*)

PATRICK. It's all going to take place at six-thirty and this room will be the scene of the crime, I suppose.

PHILLIPA. This is a crazy story, Letty, it just doesn't make sense. If someone intends to commit a murder, why on earth announce it in a newspaper for everyone to see? I should have thought it would have been wise to keep quiet about it.

JULIA. You're right, Phillipa. It's crazy. It's got to be a mad man.

PATRICK. What about a mad woman?

PHILLIPA. It's a wonder the police haven't been round here.

MISS BLACKLOCK. I shouldn't think for one moment they take it seriously.

PHILLIPA. Do you?

(A moment passes. Clearly, **MISS BLACKLOCK** *is worried.)*

MISS BLACKLOCK. *(putting on a brave face)* Of course not. It's too silly for words.

PHILLIPA. You don't sound too sure of yourself.

MISS BLACKLOCK. I certainly am! It's – it's just someone who wants an excuse for a drink. Let's forget it, shall we?

PATRICK. Poor Aunt Letty. It's rather getting on top of you, isn't it?

*(***MISS BLACKLOCK** *turns on him sharply.)*

MISS BLACKLOCK. No, it isn't! But you keep going on about it. It's stupid and childish and I've heard enough. Do you understand?

*(***MISS BLACKLOCK** *has gone over the top. The three young people stare at her – aware that she is very rattled.* **MISS BLACKLOCK** *realizes that she has gone too far and tries to cover up.)*

(The Main Door opens and **BUNNY** *enters.)*

BUNNY. Quack! Quack!

(They all turn and stare at her.)

Quack! Quack! *(She stops and looks at them.)* Quack!

*(***PATRICK** *gets the giggles and the girls stifle laughs.)*

MISS BLACKLOCK. *(covering a smile)* Is anything wrong, Bunny?

BUNNY. Infernal noise they make, Letty. They're all out on the back lawn.

MISS BLACKLOCK. Oh, my goodness – the ducks. They should have been locked up ages ago. *(suddenly, sharply)* Have you been outside like that?

BUNNY. What, Letty?

MISS BLACKLOCK. Without a coat.

BUNNY. *(guiltily)* Only to the bottom of the garden – to throw some rubbish away...

MISS BLACKLOCK. Dr. Robinson would be very annoyed – and I'm not sure I shan't tell him!

BUNNY. Please don't...

MISS BLACKLOCK. You'll be the death of me! *(She suddenly realizes what she has said. Embarrassed.)* I – I'd better lock them up. I'll only be a minute.

PHILLIPA. I'll do it.

MISS BLACKLOCK. Certainly not, Phillipa. You've been at work all day. You relax.

PATRICK. I'll go.

MISS BLACKLOCK. Thank you, Patrick. But I'd rather do it myself.

(MISS BLACKLOCK exits through the Main Door.)

BUNNY. If I'd had my goloshes on I would have done it for her.

PATRICK. I noticed you stayed discreetly in the background. Afraid of getting your hands dirty?

JULIA. No. My new dress, as a matter of fact. *(She spins round to show off her skirt which is a beautiful and clearly expensive kilt.)*

PHILLIPA. That must have cost a bomb.

JULIA. A *friend* bought it for me...

PHILLIPA. Oh – like that, is it?

JULIA. Ask no questions...

PATRICK. *(imitating the Man in the Black Voice)* Death wore Black Chiffon.

JULIA. I beg your pardon.

PATRICK. If you're the murderer – Death wore Black Chiffon would be very appropriate, wouldn't it?

JULIA. If you're trying to be funny...

(**BUNNY** *interrupts before* **JULIA** *can finish.*)

BUNNY. I once read a book called that.

PHILLIPA. Are you sure, Bunny?

BUNNY. No. No, that wasn't it. Let me see. It was called – *Death Wore Black Lingerie.*

(They all look at her in amazement. She looks up at them smiling benignly.)

(After a moment of thought.) No, no. I'm wrong. *Death Wore a Bra and Panties.* That's it. Definitely. Nice book – though there were some parts that I didn't quite understand. *(She beams at them.)*

(The Main Doors open and **MISS BLACKLOCK** *enters.)*

MISS BLACKLOCK. There is something you can do for me, Patrick.

PATRICK. Anything.

MISS BLACKLOCK. *(going to the drinks)* There's not much sherry. *(She picks up a bottle.)* Put this away and get a new one please.

(**PATRICK** *looks at the bottle, puzzled.*)

PATRICK. There's more than half a bottle.

MISS BLACKLOCK. It's been open a long time…

(She hands the bottle to him. He takes the bottle and looks at it, even more puzzled.)

PATRICK. But… *(He checks himself and goes to the door.)*

(As **PATRICK** *reaches the Main Door it opens and* **MITZI** *enters. She stands there like an usher about to make an announcement.)*

MITZI. *(trying to be dignified)* Here are Mrs. Swettenham and her son Edmund Swettenham. Thank you. You're welcome.

(**JULIA** *has to turn her back.* **PHILLIPA** *just manages to keep a straight face.* **PATRICK** *laughs.* **MITZI** *is furious.*)

Why you laugh at me?

PATRICK. *(controlling himself)* It wasn't you – it was something else – honest.

MITZI. You – you keep out of my kitchen!

MISS BLACKLOCK. Mitzi!

(**MITZI** *turns, and almost knocks the* **SWETTENHAMS** *flying as she exits.*)

MITZI. This way, please.

(**MITZI** *exits.* **MRS. SWETTENHAM** *and* **EDMUND** *enter. She is a woman in her late fifties. He is twenty-six or twenty-seven, a serious young man with pretensions of being a writer. He has not had anything published yet. He is dark and somewhat foreign-looking, although he is, in fact, very English.*)

(**MISS BLACKLOCK.** *moves up to greet them.*)

MISS BLACKLOCK. Clara. Edmund. How nice of you to call.

MRS. SWETTENHAM. *(awkwardly)* We were – just passing – Letty...

MISS BLACKLOCK. *Really?*

MRS. SWETTENHAM. That's right – isn't it, Edmund?

(*She turns to* **EDMUND** *for support, but clearly his heart is not in it.*)

EDMUND. Yes, Mother – that's right.

(**PATRICK** *exits through the Main Door.*)

MRS. SWETTENHAM. We were in the car and I said to Edmund – who drives much too fast, you know – "Oh, look, Edmund. We're passing Little Paddocks. Letty would never forgive us if we didn't drop in and say hello." And Edmund said... (*She turns to him again.*) What was it you said?

(*He swallows hard. Clearly, he is embarrassed.*)

EDMUND. "What a good idea."

MRS. SWETTENHAM. And I said – "Yes, isn't it." So, here we are.

MISS BLACKLOCK. Well, it was very nice of you to think of us. Do sit down. *(To* **BUNNY.***)* Isn't it, Bunny?

BUNNY. What is, Letty?

MISS BLACKLOCK. Clara and Edmund were just passing and decided to drop in and see how we were.

BUNNY. Oh, but this morning you said they'd be bound to call in – bursting with curiosity you said – after seeing the announcement in the *Gazette.* You did see it, didn't you, Clara?

(If the ground could open up and swallow all of them, it would be merciful.)

MRS. SWETTENHAM. Well, I er – that is – was it the one...

BUNNY. Right at the bottom of the Personal Column...

*(***PATRICK*** enters with a bottle of sherry.)*

MRS. SWETTENHAM. Oh, yes. I may have noticed it... *(She gives a nervous little laugh.)*

BUNNY. Julia said you'd be here, too. Wild horses, wouldn't keep you away...

*(***MRS. SWETTENHAM*** and **JULIA*** smile sweetly at each other. ***MISS BLACKLOCK*** attempts to ease the embarrassment.)*

MISS BLACKLOCK. Well, anyway – now that you are here...

PATRICK. *(picking up)* Totally unexpected.

MISS BLACKLOCK. *(glaring at him)* Patrick! Er – let's all have a drink.

PATRICK. Um?

MISS BLACKLOCK. *Drinks.*

PATRICK. *(waking up)* Yes, of course. Sherry, Mrs. Swettenham?

*(***MISS BLACKLOCK*** leads **MRS. SWETTENHAM*** and **EDMUND*** across to the bay window.)*

MRS. SWETTENHAM. *(still a little put out)* Well, um – yes, that will be fine, thank you.

PATRICK. Edmund?

EDMUND. Thank you.

> *(PATRICK busies himself at the sideboard getting drinks for everyone. EDMUND, still embarrassed, turns his attention to PHILLIPA.)*

Well, Phillipa. You looked very busy this morning.

PHILLIPA. Things got even more hectic after you left.

JULIA. *(seizing on it)* I see. You two have been having *secret* meetings, eh? *Hatching* something?

PHILLIPA. *(seething)* There was nothing *secret* about it and we're not hatching anything.

EDMUND. *(still embarrassed)* No, no. By no means. You see, I had to call at Dayas Hall with some honey for Mrs. Lucas.

JULIA. That's *your story.*

PHILLIPA. Julia...

JULIA. Yes, darling?

PHILLIPA. I should be careful. Otherwise a few things might come out that the rest of us would consider most peculiar...

> *(PATRICK steps in fast with the drinks to stop a storm blowing up.)*

PATRICK. Drinks, everyone!

> *(PATRICK hands MRS. SWETTENHAM and EDMUND their drinks; then MISS BLACKLOCK and BUNNY. He hands a glass each to JULIA and PHILLIPA.)*

Cheers!

> *(They take their drinks, still angry with one another and are about to drink.)*

I've laced yours with a dash of cyanide!

> *(This stops them in mid-action, but PATRICK raises his glass to them and to the others. The others return his greeting but the two girls are still a bit dubious. Then JULIA decides to take the plunge.)*

JULIA. Oh, well – you can only die once. Cheers!

(JULIA *drinks and* PHILLIPA *follows her example.*
JULIA *indicates to them to move back to the main part
of the drawing-room. While they are taking up various
positions in the room,* MISS BLACKLOCK *crosses to
the cigarette-box on the small table.* PATRICK *remains
near the drinks.* BUNNY *goes to her chair, which is
positioned so that she is in the best possible place to see*
MISS BLACKLOCK. PHILLIPA *and* EDMUND *move so
that they are in a direct line with the Main Door.* MISS
BLACKLOCK *crosses to* PHILLIPA *with the cigarette-box.*
PHILLIPA *takes one and* EDMUND *lights it for her with
a match.*)

BUNNY. Letty?

MISS BLACKLOCK. Yes?

BUNNY. When is this murder going to take place?

MRS. SWETTENHAM. Six-thirty… (*She realizes she has jumped
in too quickly for someone who was "just passing" and not
too concerned.*)

BUNNY. (*to* MRS. SWETTENHAM) Are you the murderer?

(MRS. SWETTENHAM *is startled by* BUNNY's *directness
– so is everyone else.*)

MRS. SWETTENHAM. Me? Of course I'm not?

BUNNY. Well, you seem to know all about it.

MRS. SWETTENHAM. (*flustered*) Well, er – it was in the *Gazette*
– wasn't it?

MISS BLACKLOCK. (*helping out*) I wouldn't be surprised if
everyone in Chipping Cleghorn saw it this morning.

MRS. SWETTENHAM. (*thankfully*) Yes – yes, indeed…

(MISS BLACKLOCK *indicates the clock.*)

MISS BLACKLOCK. It's nearly six-thirty, and if it's going
to happen at all it'll be any moment now. Cigarette,
anyone?

MRS. SWETTENHAM. No, thank you.

PHILLIPA. Yes please, Letty.

(MISS BLACKLOCK crosses to PHILLIPA and offers a cigarette to PHILLIPA who takes one. EDMUND lights it for her.)

Thank you, Edmund.

(The clock starts to chime the half-hour. All eyes turn to look at it. Everybody freezes; transfixed by the clock. We can almost feel the tension. As the last chime rings out, the lights go out leaving the room in total darkness.)

(We hear BUNNY gasp – almost a scream. One or two voices speak out: "What's happening?," "Who'sput the lights out?" "Come on – you've had your joke. Put them back on.," "For goodness sake, stop playing around. It's not funny anymore.," and so on.)

(Then the Main Door bursts open with a crash, and a powerful flashlight plays round the room. The man holding the flashlight is RUDI SCHERZ – a young Swiss national.)

SCHERZ. *(barking)* Get your hands up! Stay where you are!

(The flashlight lands on JULIA… Her hands are still by her side – she is very cool.)

(More angrily.) I said: Get your hands up! If you want to get out of this alive do as you're told.

(His tone of voice is such that JULIA obeys instantly. The flashlight moves on to MRS. SWETTENHAM who gives a startled gasp, but whose hands would touch the ceiling if she could make them do so. The light now swings on to EDMUND – but he has made only a half hearted attempt to obey the order.)

You! High! High above your head!

(The menace in this man's voice leaves no doubt in EDMUND's mind. His hands shoot up. BUNNY is shaking with fear and is out of her chair and standing on tip-toe in an effort to do as she is told. The light swings from her and lands on PATRICK who, for once, is behaving himself.)

You, away from the door. Go.

(The light stays on **PATRICK** *briefly and then moves on to just about where* **MISS BLACKLOCK** *is standing.)*

Now!

(At this point, we hear firstly two shots fired – then a tiny pause – followed by a third shot. There are several screams, then, the flashlight falls to the ground and spins round before going out, and at the same time we hear a heavy thud. Then there is silence, held for a moment until **JULIA** *breaks it.)*

JULIA. For God's sake. Someone put the lights on!

MRS. SWETTENHAM. Has he gone?

PHILLIPA. I can't see – have you got those matches Edmund?

*(***EDMUND** *searches for a moment.)*

EDMUND. Blast! That was the last one.

MRS. SWETTENHAM. Someone put the lights on…

PATRICK. They must be fused.

EDMUND. Where's the fuse-box?

PATRICK. In the hall – I'll go.

(We hear **PATRICK** *cross the room and stumble.)*

What the hell?

JULIA. What is it?

PATRICK. Stay calm. I'll soon have the lights back on.

*(***PATRICK** *exits through the Main Door.)*

BUNNY. *(tremulously)* Letty… *(She waits for a moment or two – there is no reply.)* Letty…?

MISS BLACKLOCK. It's all right, Bunny – stay calm.

BUNNY. I'm frightened…

MISS BLACKLOCK. *(strained)* There's no need…

(A moment, and then the Lights come on.)

EDMUND. He's unconscious. Must have knocked himself out.

(**PATRICK** *enters.*)

PATRICK. Who is it?

EDMUND. I've no idea. Better get his gun – before he comes round.

PATRICK. Yes... (*He spots the gun by* **RUDI SCHERZ,** *and is about to pick it up but checks himself. He takes a handkerchief from his pocket and picks the gun up by the barrel.*)

MISS BLACKLOCK. Will someone please help me.

(*All eyes turn to* **MISS BLACKLOCK** *and ignore the body of* **RUDI SCHERZ** *on the floor.* **MISS BLACKLOCK** *has blood all down the side of her face and all over her white blouse. It is a very dramatic sight so it is easy for them all to ignore* **SCHERZ** *for the moment.*)

BUNNY. (*horrified*) Letty...

(*Everyone moves to her as she sways unsteadily on her feet. They crowd round her, firing questions: "Is she badly hurt?" "It looks terrible.," "Someone get her a brandy.," and so on.*)

PHILLIPA. Brandy? We'd better call a doctor.

MISS BLACKLOCK. No! I shall be all right...

(*At the same time we hear banging on a door offstage and* **MITZI** *screaming – but quite distant. No one takes any notice at this stage.* **JULIA** *and* **PHILLIPA** *help* **MISS BLACKLOCK** *to a chair.*)

MISS BLACKLOCK. It's nothing – just my ear...

(**EDMUND** *notices* **PATRICK** *holding the gun in the handkerchief.*)

EDMUND. Why the handkerchief?

PATRICK. (*indignantly*) I don't suppose the police would be very happy if I got my fingerprints all over it.

MRS. SWETTENHAM. Police?

EDMUND. They'll have to be called in, mother.

(*The banging on the door and the shouting off continues.* **PHILLIPA** *turns to it.*)

PHILLIPA. Is that Mitzi?

PATRICK. Yes. Someone seems to have locked her in the dining room.

PHILLIPA. Why do that?

PATRICK. I've no idea.

PHILLIPA. Hadn't we better let her out?

JULIA. I'll do it.

PATRICK. No. There might be a… I'll do it in a moment.

MRS. SWETTENHAM. Are you feeling better, Letty?

MISS BLACKLOCK. *(with a thin smile)* Thank you…

(**MISS MARPLE** *enters, with* **MITZI** *close behind.*)

MISS MARPLE. What happened?

JULIA. Aunt Letty's been shot at.

(**MISS MARPLE** *bends down to examine* **RUDI SCHERZ,** *who is at her feet.*)

MISS MARPLE. By this man?

(**PATRICK** *moves to her and the body.* **MITZI** *is frozen to the spot.*)

PATRICK. Of course! Is he coming round?

MISS MARPLE. *(looking up)* No.

PATRICK. I wonder who he is?

MISS MARPLE. I know who he is.

(*They all turn to look at* **MISS MARPLE.**)

His name is Rudi Scherz – *(pause)* – and he's dead!

(curtain)

Scene III

(The same. The following Saturday morning.)

(As the curtain goes up, **INSPECTOR CRADDOCK** *is lying in the same position as the body in the previous scene.* **SERGEANT MELLORS** *is standing below the sideboard looking at* **CRADDOCK**. **CRADDOCK**, *a man of about fifty, rises and looks at the bullet holes in the wall by the sideboard.)*

CRADDOCK. So. He fires two shots from here – hits the wall – and then shoots himself?

MELLORS. If he tripped, he could have done it accidentally, sir.

CRADDOCK. Are they all here, now?

MELLORS. Yes, sir. Grumbling and moaning…

CRADDOCK. *(with apparent uninterest)* Oh…

MELLORS. And I should watch that Edmund Swettenham.

CRADDOCK. Why?

MELLORS. I should think he's a bit of a left-wing intellectual.

CRADDOCK. I didn't get that impression last night.

MELLORS. He's been a bit bolshy with me, sir. He was having a go at the Force this morning. Sprouting on about our Gestapo methods.

CRADDOCK. Oh – Christ! Why do I always pick the awkward ones?

MELLORS. You do seem to attract them, sir.

CRADDOCK. Why can't I get a nice, peaceful, law-abiding lot who do as they're told and answer my questions with a certain amount of civility.

MELLORS. Not your style, sir.

CRADDOCK. Once! Just once! That's all I ask. *(He looks up, pointing.)* Somebody up there doesn't like me, Sergeant. And, what's more – *(indicating off)* – that lot out there are trying to compound the felony.

MELLORS. *(after a moment)* Shall I wheel them in?

CRADDOCK. There's nothing else for it, is there?

MELLORS. 'Fraid not, sir.

*(**MELLORS** goes to the Locked Door and tries to open it.)*

CRADDOCK. Not that door, it's been sealed for years.

*(**MELLORS** goes out through the Main Door and across to the dining-room, asking the people to come through into the drawing-room. They do so, everyone who was in the room at the close of the previous scene, chattering amongst themselves as they enter)*

(In a normal voice.) Can I have your attention, please?

(They take no notice.)

Quiet, please.

(They still take no notice.)

(Shouting.) Perlease!

(They are all a little taken aback. The chatter dies instantly.)

That's very good of you. I do appreciate your co-operation.

MRS. SWETTENHAM. This is very inconvenient, Inspector. It is Saturday. There's shopping, and lots of jobs to be done.

CRADDOCK. I understand your problem, Mrs. Swettenham. But, may I remind you, a man died here last night – right on the spot where you're standing –

*(A little horrified at the thought, **MRS. SWETTENHAM** shifts her position.)*

– and whilst it may not seem overly important to you – it is to me and society in general. So, if it's not asking too much I'd like you to push your shopping to the back of your mind for a while and answer a few questions.

EDMUND. *(irritatedly)* I would have thought there were enough questions asked last night...

CRADDOCK. Ah, well – perhaps you don't think the same way as me, young man. Yes, I should think that's the answer – we think differently. But, if you cast your mind back – way, way back to last night – you'll surely recall that I allowed you all to go home and get some rest on the understanding that you'd co-operate fully this morning.

EDMUND. Well, it's perfectly clear what happened. This man – Scherz was his name, I believe –

CRADDOCK. Yes.

EDMUND. – broke in here – intending to steal – from Miss Blacklock – or the rest of us – fired the shots to scare us – tripped in the dark – and killed himself, poor devil.

(CRADDOCK *eyes him for a moment.*)

CRADDOCK. I understand you're a bit of a writer?

EDMUND. *(embarrassedly)* Well, er – yes – I do write...

CRADDOCK. Well, I hope all your plots aren't as obvious as that – otherwise I don't think I'll be very interested in reading any of your books!

(JULIA *stifles a laugh.*)

Now, er – perhaps we could get on with this –

MISS BLACKLOCK. I'm sure we're all perfectly willing to do anything you ask, Inspector. But, it has been quite a shock to us, you know...

CRADDOCK. I appreciate that, Miss Blacklock. But, you see, for a start – he didn't break in. No locks broken. No windows forced...

MISS MARPLE. He must have come in by the back door – I did.

CRADDOCK. *(to MISS BLACKLOCK)* And, as I was saying when Miss Marple interrupted me, there's your very bad habit of leaving the doors unlocked for *all and sundry* to come and go as they please.

MISS BLACKLOCK. I locked the front door –

CRADDOCK. For once...

MISS BLACKLOCK. – and everyone in the village does it – leaves them open, I mean.

CRADDOCK. Foolish – very foolish.

MISS BLACKLOCK. I suppose I must have left the back door open when I went to lock up the ducks...

CRADDOCK. Now, Miss Blacklock, last night you said you knew this Rudi Scherz.

MISS BLACKLOCK. Hardly knew, Inspector. His father owned a small hotel in Montreux. I spent many years in Switzerland helping to nurse my sister and I used to have a meal there occasionally. Recently, I had lunch in The Royal Spa Hotel in Medenham Wells. He was there. He approached me – said he recognized me and that he was over here to get a thorough grounding in the hotel business. However, I must point out that I had no recollection of him at all. But a few days later he called on me here...

CRADDOCK. He's been here before?

MISS BLACKLOCK. Yes.

BUNNY. I remember, Letty. You were very upset. He asked you for some money.

MISS BLACKLOCK. That's right. He gave me some story about his father being taken seriously ill and he desperately needed money for his air fare. Well I believed he was lying. After all, if his father owned a hotel, surely his family could afford to send him the fare? I told him I had no intention of lending him money. What surprised me most was that he didn't make a fuss. He just left – like a lamb.

CRADDOCK. I see. Do you think he may have called here purely to look around? See what the layout of the house was? That sort of thing.

MISS BLACKLOCK. Well. I haven't given it much thought – until now. I suppose that's what he must have been up to. Not that it would have done him any good. I don't keep more than a few pounds in the house.

CRADDOCK. Valuables?

MISS BLACKLOCK. Nothing.

CRADDOCK. Jewellery? Silver?

MISS BLACKLOCK. Nothing worth a great deal. Little bits and pieces. The silver's reasonable – nothing more. Mitzi was cleaning it last night…

*(**MITZI** instantly springs to life.)*

MITZI. I not touch it! It is nothing to you Secret Police officers. You come here. You blame me all the time. It was the same where I come from. Torture. Interrogation. But, I do not crack. You understand. I do not break. I tell them nothing. *(She stamps her foot and stands there defiantly with her hands on her hips.)* Yah!

*(**CRADDOCK** stands there for a moment, long-suffering, then appeals to the others.)*

CRADDOCK. Is she always like this?

MITZI. Torture me! You get nowhere! I am innocent! Innocent! I was locked in the dining-room. That – is my hundred-percent alibi – as you say!

CRADDOCK. And a very good alibi it is. Perhaps too good on the surface. Now just sit down. And try to remember that I'm not too keen on the histrionics…

MITZI. *(still furious)* I will not…

CRADDOCK. Ah – ah – ah! *(Firmly.)* Sit!

*(**MITZI** sits, like a lamb.)*

CRADDOCK. Let me say this to all of you. I don't want to be here anymore than you do. There's a very good football match on at Milchester this afternoon I'd very much like to see. But, other things are more – pressing. *Please.* Can we continue this interrogation without any more interruptions? Miss Blacklock. We've established that you knew Rudi Scherz.

MISS MARPLE. Excuse me, Inspector. I'm sorry to interrupt. I knew him, too.

(CRADDOCK looks along the length of his nose at her. Another interruption! MISS MARPLE smiles sweetly at him.)

CRADDOCK. You didn't mention this last night.

MISS MARPLE. I did – but, you weren't here at the time. And, well – when you arrived you rather neglected me.

CRADDOCK. Did I Oh…!

MISS MARPLE. Probably because I didn't arrive until after the, er – action – took place.

CRADDOCK. Hm – rather like turning to the end of the book to see who the killer is, eh?

(This is the start of their relationship. A rapport which builds as the story unfolds.)

MISS MARPLE. As analogy it doesn't work. Because that's cheating. I usually guess who it is without resorting to those tactics. Do you turn to the last page?

CRADDOCK. *(sniffing)* If only I could. You, er – knew Rudi Scherz, you said?

MISS MARPLE. I stayed at the Royal Spa whilst I was having intensive treatment – for rheumatism. He made up my bill.

CRADDOCK. *(knowingly)* Ah.

MISS MARPLE. There were one or two – discrepancies – which I couldn't fail to notice, of course.

CRADDOCK. Of course.

MISS MARPLE. It was clear to me that he was "on the make," as they say in the trade. Naturally, when the errors were pointed out he apologized profusely. But, we both knew.

CRADDOCK. Did you report him?

MISS MARPLE. There was nothing I could actually *prove.*

CRADDOCK. He does seem to have been a bit of a villain. I'll know more soon. The Swiss police are running a check on him. *(pause)* I'd like you all to take up the exact positions you were in last night as far as possible, that is – when the shots were fired.

MISS MARPLE. Do you want me to leave? I was coming up the drive.

CRADDOCK. So you were outside when you heard the shots were you?

MISS MARPLE. I was, Inspector. As you will realize I came in through the back door. Mitzi was banging about in the dining-room. I let her out and then we both came in here.

CRADDOCK. Tell you what you can do. Keep an eye on her. I don't want her banging about again.

MITZI. *(bristling)* I am not banging about – *(she carries on in Hungarian)* – mindig en vagyok a hibd's...

CRADDOCK. Shush – shush – shush...!

MITZI. Ah...

CRADDOCK. And shush again!

(**MISS MARPLE** *takes* **MITZI** *by the arm and leads her to the sofa by the window.*)

MISS MARPLE. Come and sit down, Mitzi...

CRADDOCK. Now come along everyone, perlease.

(The others now start to take up their positions.)

Thank you. Thank you very much. *(He goes to the Main Door.)* The lights go out – and a flashlight comes on, then lands on – you! *(He points to* **JULIA.***)*

JULIA. My hands weren't up. I thought it was a joke. Then he – barked at me. I was so frightened I put my hands up so high – like this... *(She demonstrates.)*

CRADDOCK. He couldn't complain at that, could he?

(**JULIA** *drops her hands.*)

JULIA. I thought he was going to shoot me.

CRADDOCK. You're Miss Blacklock's niece. Right?

JULIA. *(puzzled and hesitant)* Well – yes...

CRADDOCK. That's the sort of answer I like. Full of confidence. You *are* Miss Blacklock's niece?

JULIA. *(indignantly)* It's just that I don't see what my relationship with Aunt Letty has to do with it.

CRADDOCK. May I suggest that you leave me to work that out? In any case. I was merely trying to establish who you are.

JULIA. You can check up on it if you like.

CRADDOCK. I will. Your mother lives in the south of France I understand?

JULIA. *(nervously)* She's lived there for some time. It suits her health.

CRADDOCK. *(after a moment)* Thank you. Mrs. Swettenham?

MRS. SWETTENHAM. Yes?

(They regard each other for a brief moment.)

CRADDOCK. The light moved on to you next, Mrs. Swettenham?

MRS. SWETTENHAM. I was totally dazzled. I couldn't see anything. I just heard that voice – frightening – gutteral...

CRADDOCK. You haven't all that long returned to this country. Is that right?

MRS. SWETTENHAM. Yes. My husband was in the Diplomatic Service. He died abroad. Naturally, I returned with Edmund...

CRADDOCK. Where were you – abroad, that is?

MRS. SWETTENHAM. *(bothered)* Why? Turin. My husband was with the Trade Delegation there. *(Clearly worried by this line of interrogation.)* I don't see what my personal life has got to do with this.

(CRADDOCK ignores her last remark.)

CRADDOCK. If my knowledge of geography hasn't entirely deserted me – Turin is not all that far from the Swiss border, is it?

MRS. SWETTENHAM. No.

CRADDOCK. Thank you, Mrs. Swettenham.

(EDMUND springs to her defense.)

EDMUND. Just what are you insinuating?

(**CRADDOCK** *turns slowly to face him, and looks at him for a moment.*)

CRADDOCK. The light fell on you next, didn't it?

EDMUND. *(very definitely)* Yes, it did!

CRADDOCK. Thank you very much.

(*With this he turns and ignores him.*)

EDMUND. Aren't you going to ask me any more questions?

CRADDOCK. Not right now. (*He turns back to face* **PHILLIPA.**) Mrs. Haymes. The light never fell on you at all, did it?

PHILLIPA. No, it didn't.

CRADDOCK. You were actually facing the door.

PHILLIPA. That's right...

CRADDOCK. Was it possible to see this man at all?

PHILLIPA. Not really – it was difficult to see anything.

CRADDOCK. But, you were in a good position.

PHILLIPA. It was very dark – I suppose I could make out a shape – but nothing more.

CRADDOCK. *(after a moment)* How long ago did your husband die?

(*This question seems to throw* **PHILLIPA.**)

PHILLIPA. *(startled)* Why? What on earth has it got to do with this?

CRADDOCK. I'd like to know when and why you came to live here.

PHILLIPA. I still don't see what the relevance is...

(**CRADDOCK** *moves so that he is closer to her. Clearly, it makes her feel uneasy.*)

CRADDOCK. Does it strike you as odd that virtually all of you are *newcomers* to Chipping Cleghorn?

(*A moment. They all feel a little uncomfortable.*)

PHILLIPA. It's – never occurred to me until now.

CRADDOCK. Odd though...

PHILLIPA. I came here a few months ago because I was offered a job. Restoring the gardens at Dayas Hall. I'm a trained horticulturist.

CRADDOCK. That's nice. Gardener! *(He turns his attention to* **BUNNY.***)* Miss Bunner.

BUNNY. You've not going to give me the third degree are you, Inspector?

CRADDOCK. *(smiling)* Not today. But, if you can tell me what you saw – if anything – I'd be very grateful. You were in a good position to see Miss Blacklock and the gunman if the lights had been on.

BUNNY. *(pleased)* Yes, I was.

CRADDOCK. I want you to think very hard and tell me what you saw *before* the lights went out.

BUNNY. Before?

CRADDOCK. Yes. Then we'll see what you remember after the lights went out.

BUNNY. Let me see – Letty was holding the vase…

MISS BLACKLOCK. No, Bunny, dear. I was holding the cigarette-box. I'd been handing them round.

*(***BUNNY*** looks puzzled.)*

BUNNY. *(thoughtfully)* I remember now. You were holding the cigarette-box, not the vase.

CRADDOCK. Then what, Miss Bunner?

BUNNY. The flash…

CRADDOCK. From the torch?

BUNNY. No…

CRADDOCK. Oh?

BUNNY. There was a flash. It must have been the light on the cigarette-box. We always keep it polished.

CRADDOCK. Ah…

BUNNY. Then it was dark – and he fired his gun at poor Letty. How could anyone do that?

CRADDOCK. You actually saw him fire the gun?

BUNNY. I saw the gun fire at Letty.

CRADDOCK. Thank you, Miss Bunner.

BUNNY. He should be locked up.

JULIA. Bunny, he's dead.

BUNNY. Serves him right. He tried to murder Letty.

(**CRADDOCK** *moves to* **PATRICK.**)

CRADDOCK. *You* were by the door. Having a few drinks?

PATRICK. I only had one, you know.

CRADDOCK. Whatever you say. But, you were by the door.

PATRICK. No. I was by the door but he told me to move away from it. After the first two shots, he brushed past me and I tried to trip him up.

CRADDOCK. That's when you think he fell?

PATRICK. Yes, I suppose so.

CRADDOCK. And after that you went out to mend the fuse?

PATRICK. Yes. I didn't mend it. I simply switched the fuses around. It was quicker and easier. It was easy for me, of course. I knew exactly where the fuse-box was – how to open it – and which circuit was affected… (*He trails off.*)

(*A moment's pause.* **PATRICK** *licks his lips nervously.*)

CRADDOCK. You're Miss Simmons' brother?

PATRICK. (*still nervously*) Um – I'm a year older…

CRADDOCK. Miss Blacklock's nephew?

PATRICK. Er, no…

CRADDOCK. I understood you were.

MISS BLACKLOCK. We're second cousins, Inspector. Patrick's mother is my first cousin…

PATRICK. We call her Aunt because our mother always referred to her as that… So, when we came to live here – (*he shrugs his shoulders*) – well…

CRADDOCK. How long have you been living here?

PATRICK. Three months – I should think.

CRADDOCK. So the three of you have only really known each other since about June or July this year?

MISS BLACKLOCK. I did know them as children...

CRADDOCK. Mmm. I see. *(To* MISS BLACKLOCK.*)* Would you mind standing in the exact position you were in when the shots were fired, please?

*(*MISS BLACKLOCK *looks at the wall, shuffles her feet and checks again to see that she is in position.* CRADDOCK *moves to her and traces the path the bullet would have taken before it entered the wall. He does it for each hole. We see that one could very easily have nicked her ear.)*

Well. That was a very narrow escape, wasn't it?

MISS BLACKLOCK. I was extremely fortunate.

*(*CRADDOCK *turns from her to address the others.)*

CRADDOCK. Right. Well, that wasn't too painful, was it?

JULIA. We can go?

CRADDOCK. You can. But, do all stay in the village, won't you? Don't take a sudden and unexpected holiday or anything like that.

MISS MARPLE. Excuse me, Inspector?

CRADDOCK. Yes, Miss Marple?

MISS MARPLE. You haven't questioned me.

CRADDOCK. But, you didn't turn up until after the, er – action!

MISS MARPLE. *(a tinge indignantly)* Suppose I was lying? Suppose I was Rudi Scherz' accomplice? I could easily have locked Mitzi in the dining-room. I could have hidden for a while – I know the layout of the house – then pretended to turn up after it was all over?

CRADDOCK. In that case, I'll put you under arrest!

MISS MARPLE. *(astonished)* But, I didn't – and I wasn't his accomplice!

CRADDOCK. In that case, you're free to go!

*(*MISS MARPLE *is irritated that he has been getting at her – teasing her.)*

MISS MARPLE. How very disappointing. You're having a game with me, Inspector.

CRADDOCK. And you with me, Miss Marple. I shall question you – when I'm ready.

MISS MARPLE. Very well.

CRADDOCK. Thank you everyone – I shall be talking to you all again soon. Miss Blacklock, I'd like you to stay.

(Everyone files out except **CRADDOCK** *and* **MISS MARPLE.***)*

Sit down, please, Miss Blacklock.

*(***MISS BLACKLOCK*** *goes to a chair, clearly a little nervous. He moves to sit opposite her. A moment, as they sit facing each other. A little tension starting to creep in.)*

(Seriously.) Miss Blacklock…

MISS BLACKLOCK. *(nervously)* Yes…

CRADDOCK. I think it's cards on the table time.

MISS BLACKLOCK. *(warily)* I don't understand, Inspector.

CRADDOCK. I think you do.

(Another moment passes – more tension builds up.)

Someone tried to kill you last night.

MISS BLACKLOCK. *(exclaiming)* Oh no! No, Inspector!

CRADDOCK. I think there's no doubt of it.

MISS BLACKLOCK. But, *why?*

CRADDOCK. I hope we're going to find out.

MISS BLACKLOCK. I think you're wrong, Inspector. There were plenty of opportunities for Rudi Scherz to kill me if he wanted to. Why wait till last night? Why invite witnesses?

CRADDOCK. What makes you think it was Rudi Scherz?

MISS BLACKLOCK. Well – wasn't it?

CRADDOCK. He did place the advertisement in the *Gazette*.

MISS BLACKLOCK. Well, there you are. It sort of – proves my point. If he'd wanted to kill me, why not wait behind a hedge and pop me off when no one was about? No, I'm sorry, Inspector. I think you're wrong. He didn't come here to kill me.

(pause)

CRADDOCK. Someone could have put him up to it.

MISS BLACKLOCK. *(puzzled)* Put him up to it?

CRADDOCK. Someone who wanted you dead – and is prepared to pay Rudi Scherz to do the job. You see, I'm not so sure *his* death was an accident.

MISS BLACKLOCK. How could it be anything else? He tripped and shot himself.

CRADDOCK. No. Supposing there was someone else. And what if this someone assumed that he'd done his job and killed you? Wouldn't it be safer to shoot Rudi Scherz so that there was no possibility of him getting caught by the police and telling us the truth?

MISS BLACKLOCK. I see exactly what you are saying, Inspector.

CRADDOCK. You agree with me then?

MISS BLACKLOCK. No. Because *why!* Why should anyone want to kill me.

CRADDOCK. I've a feeling you might be able to answer that.

MISS BLACKLOCK. I can't. I've no enemies that I know of. I'm on friendly terms with everyone in the village. It's too ridiculous.

(There is a pause. CRADDOCK considers his next move.)

CRADDOCK. Who gets your money if you die?

(MISS BLACKLOCK takes a deep breath.)

MISS BLACKLOCK. Is this *really* necessary, Inspector?

CRADDOCK. Perlease, Miss Blacklock. Indulge me. Answer my question.

(She considers for a moment.)

MISS BLACKLOCK. *(reluctantly)* Patrick and Julia…

CRADDOCK. I see.

MISS BLACKLOCK. *(angrily)* I might add that the furniture and a small annuity goes to – Miss Bunner. So I suppose she becomes a suspect, too! The point is – there really isn't much to leave. Frankly, I'm not *worth* murdering.

CRADDOCK. But, nevertheless, all *three* of them benefit.

MISS BLACKLOCK. And not *one* of them would harm a hair on my head!

CRADDOCK. You'd be surprised what people will do for money.

(MISS BLACKLOCK loses her cool. She gets up and moves away from him in an attempt to bring the interview to an end.)

MISS BLACKLOCK. Really, Inspector – I find this conversation extremely distasteful. You are accusing people very dear to me. People I trust – yes, with my life!

(There is a pause. Each is wary of the other.)

CRADDOCK. Have you got anything of great value?

MISS BLACKLOCK. *(irritatedly)* Nothing special – nothing out of the ordinary...

CRADDOCK. *(indicating)* Those pearls you're wearing?

(MISS BLACKLOCK's hand goes up to her throat in a reflex action – just to touch them for a second.)

MISS BLACKLOCK. They *are priceless*...

CRADDOCK. *(on his toes)* Oh?

MISS BLACKLOCK. But only to me. They belong to my sister. We were very close. I wear them all the time. They somehow – and I don't suppose you'll understand this for one minute – keep me in touch with her...

CRADDOCK. *(after a moment)* I like to think I'm not insensitive. But, I still think someone is trying to kill you. Can you come back to the wall, please.

(They go to the wall where the bullets entered.)

If he'd merely intended to frighten you and everyone else, he could have fired the shots into the ceiling. But, think. The clock struck the half-hour. Everybody turned to it. The lights went out. The door swung open...

(As he says this, the Main Door starts to swing open. **MISS BLACKLOCK** *gasps.* **CRADDOCK**'s *jaw drops open.)*

(Finally, the Main Door swings fully open to reveal – **MISS MARPLE**, *who is standing there with a toy gun in one hand and a torch in the other.)*

MISS BLACKLOCK. Miss Marple!

*(***MISS MARPLE*** *moves into the room, looking quite menacing.)*

CRADDOCK. Give me that gun!

MISS MARPLE. It's a toy. It fires pieces of potato.

CRADDOCK. What is this all about?

MISS MARPLE. I couldn't help wondering how that young man could be in three places at once – fusing the lights, locking Mitzi in the dining-room and opening the door with a gun in one hand and a torch in the other. I couldn't. I had to put the gun down, open the door and pick it up after. It seems to me he was a very athletic young man.

CRADDOCK. Good point, Miss Marple.

MISS MARPLE. Inspector – that's praise indeed. Tell me, do you think it's possible that Rudi Scherz had an accomplice?

CRADDOCK. Miss Marple?

MISS MARPLE. Yes?

CRADDOCK. Would you like my job?

MISS MARPLE. Yes, but I'd never make a policeman.

CRADDOCK. You think not?

MISS MARPLE. I'm not tall enough. I started on that little charade in the hope that it might help to prove my theory that Rudi Scherz came here to murder Miss Blacklock…

CRADDOCK. I've been trying to convince her of that myself. Perhaps now you'll believe that it's not the ranting of an hysterical old copper. Someone is waiting to murder you and it can happen anytime now!

MISS BLACKLOCK. Just because Miss Marple agrees with you – it doesn't mean to say you're right.

CRADDOCK. I'm trying to save your life.

MISS MARPLE. I believe that, too, Miss Blacklock.

CRADDOCK. *Somewhere* there's a reason. And *you* know it – it may be hidden deep in your mind – we've got to bring it out.

MISS BLACKLOCK. *(hesitantly)* There's no reason – I'm sure...

CRADDOCK. Perlease! Think!

MISS MARPLE. But – I understand that one day you could inherit millions.

(There is a stunned silence.)

CRADDOCK. Miss Marple?

(MISS BLACKLOCK stares at MISS MARPLE who feels more than a little uncomfortable.)

MISS MARPLE. Miss Bunner was telling me when we were having coffee in the Blue Bird Coffee House...

MISS BLACKLOCK. Trust Bunny! I shall have to do something about her!

CRADDOCK. Why have you been keeping something back from me?

MISS BLACKLOCK. It's *nothing*. It doesn't concern this case or you! In fact, it's most unlikely to happen.

CRADDOCK. Do I have to ask Miss Marple or Miss Bunner for the details?

(There is a pause. CRADDOCK is seething.)

MISS BLACKLOCK. *(coolly)* Miss Marple is referring to Randall Goedler's will.

CRADDOCK. Randall Goedler?

MISS MARPLE. He was a financier, Inspector. Very flamboyant. Hailed as a genius in the City.

MISS BLACKLOCK. He was. I was his personal secretary – for nearly twenty years. He made millions.

MISS MARPLE. But, without you it might never have happened.

MISS BLACKLOCK. You seem very well informed, Miss Marple. Why don't you tell the Inspector?

MISS MARPLE. *(embarrassed)* I'm sorry. I didn't mean to be rude.

(A moment passes. Then MISS BLACKLOCK *smiles an apology.)*

MISS BLACKLOCK. No, I'm sorry, Miss Marple. But, you know that Bunny does get things muddled. You may have got a strange version of the truth.

CRADDOCK. What is the *truth?*

MISS BLACKLOCK. I loaned Randall Goedler some money in his early days – everything I had. He was up against it – a step from losing all he'd worked for. He didn't. I more or less became a junior partner. When he died he left a fortune.

CRADDOCK. To whom?

MISS BLACKLOCK. His wife, Belle. In trust for her during her lifetime. When she dies… it comes to me.

*(*CRADDOCK *gives a long, low whistle.)*

CRADDOCK. And you believe this has nothing to do with the shooting?

MISS BLACKLOCK. How can it? Rudi Scherz didn't really know me, let alone Randall Goedler. And his will wasn't made public.

CRADDOCK. It can be looked up in Somerset House. Tell me, how does Mrs. Goedler feel towards you.

MISS BLACKLOCK. *(laughing)* I haven't seen her for years we were always great friends.

MISS MARPLE. *(tentatively)* Miss Bunner was saying that her health isn't too good at the moment.

MISS BLACKLOCK. Belle was never very strong. But, Randall always said she'd outlive us all – it wouldn't surprise me. The trouble is – well, apparently, she has difficulty remembering anything or anyone now. Poor Belle. I should go and see her. But, she lives in Scotland – and it's such a long way. You know, Inspector, I've had an excellent reason for murdering Belle for years.

CRADDOCK. So, if she dies you get everything.

MISS BLACKLOCK. Well – most of it.

CRADDOCK. *(after a brief moment)* What happens if you die before she does?

(There is a pause.)

MISS BLACKLOCK. It goes to Pip and Emma.

CRADDOCK. *Who?*

MISS BLACKLOCK. *(smiling)* Yes, it does sound funny, doesn't it? Randall had a sister – Sonia. They fell out when she married a man called Dimitri Stamfordis – he sounds Greek, but he wasn't – mid-European or somewhere. A real rogue – very handsome, mind you. Randall hated him.

CRADDOCK. So he cut Sonia out of his will?

MISS BLACKLOCK. That's quite right, Inspector, but it didn't matter. She was rich in her own right. Anyway. Belle and Randall's lawyers persuaded him to put someone else in the will in case I died before her. Very sensible. Well, the only communication we received from Sonia was a letter to Belle, two or three years after she married, saying Sonia was deliriously happy and had given birth to twins…

MISS MARPLE. Pip and Emma.

MISS BLACKLOCK. Yes. I suppose the names were some sort of joke between her and her husband. One was born just before midnight and one just after.

CRADDOCK. So, there's a young man and a young lady somewhere who stand to become millionaires.

MISS BLACKLOCK. If… *(She stops herself.)*

CRADDOCK. If you die before Belle Goedler. Does anyone know what happened to Sonia and her husband?

MISS BLACKLOCK. The last we heard they were living in Eastern Europe.

CRADDOCK. How old would Pip and Emma be now?

MISS BLACKLOCK. Twenty-five or six – something like that.

CRADDOCK. They must be found. Have you any idea that they look like?

MISS BLACKLOCK. None. There were no photographs – and even if there had been they wouldn't help us to recognize Pip and Emma now.

MISS MARPLE. What did Sonia look like? They may resemble her.

MISS BLACKLOCK. Sonia. Oh. She was dark – rather temperamental – and very attractive.

CRADDOCK. *(thoughtfully)* Pip – and Emma…

MISS MARPLE. Or Sonia, Inspector. Supposing her husband – Dimitri Stamfordis, wasn't it?

(MISS BLACKLOCK *nods agreement.*)

You said he was a rogue. Supposing he went through all her money. Clearly she'd stand to gain if you died first.

CRADDOCK. Dimitri would, too.

MISS MARPLE. Yes.

CRADDOCK. So, there are at least four people who would benefit from your death, Miss Blacklock.

MISS MARPLE. Yes.

MISS BLACKLOCK. Oh, but you can discount Patrick and Julia now. If I die before Belle Goedler they'll only get a pittance.

CRADDOCK. At this stage I don't believe in discounting *anyone.* And I'd advise you to do the same.

(The Main Door opens and **MITZI** *enters pushing the trolley with coffee and biscuits on it. Her darkness is accentuated by the black dress she is wearing. Her petiteness by the flat shoes she has on: and she is a pretty girl.)*

(The others turn to her. **MITZI** *looks at them for a moment, wondering why they are staring at her.)*

MITZI. Is anything wrong?

MISS BLACKLOCK. No.

MITZI. Then why you look at me so strange?

MISS BLACKLOCK. I hadn't realized. No Mitzi – nothing at all.

*(***MITZI** *turns to exit, but* **CRADDOCK** *stops her.)*

CRADDOCK. Just a minute, Mitzi.

MITZI. What you want, policeman?

CRADDOCK. Have you any relations in this country?

MITZI. Why you want to know?

CRADDOCK. Any family…

MITZI. My family is dead – *massacred.*

MISS MARPLE. I understood they were sent to Siberia.

MITZI. Who told you that?

MISS MARPLE. Miss Bunner…

CRADDOCK. You mean you have no one – brother – or something…

(A moment. **MITZI** *watches him cautiously.)*

MITZI. I am alone.

CRADDOCK. No English relatives? Distant cousins perhaps…

MITZI. Me? English? Huh! *(She laughs.)* If it was not so funny I would be insulted.

CRADDOCK. At some time I'll need to see all your papers…

MITZI. *(furiously)* Everything is in order! I report to the immigration authorities every three months…

CRADDOCK. Calm down. It's routine. I'm obliged to do it.

MITZI. Why you not arrest me now? You think I do this thing – this *murder.* Very well. Arrest me! *(Her hands shoot out, fists clenched.)* Put on the handcuffs!

(The Main Door opens and **BUNNY** *enters, to see* **MITZI** *holding out her hands.)*

BUNNY. Good! You're arresting her, are you Inspector?

MITZI. I don't care! Arrest me!

CRADDOCK. *(irritated)* Put your hands down – I'm not in the mood.

*(**MITZI** puts her hands down.)*

BUNNY. You should arrest her. She *stole* a cup!

MITZI. I not steal anything, you stupid old woman!

MISS BLACKLOCK. *(admonishing)* Mitzi!

MITZI. No. I don't care. She accuses me of stealing. I do not!

MISS BLACKLOCK. Bunny, what's it all about?

BUNNY. One of your favourite coffee cups, Letty. It's missing. They were on the Welsh dresser in the kitchen – and *she* won't let anyone go in there. There were six – now there are only five.

MISS BLACKLOCK. I won't be angry, Mitzi. Did you break one?

MITZI. *(her nostrils flaring)* First murder. Now stealing. And why? Because I am a foreigner. That's the truth! *(She raises an accusing finger at* **BUNNY.**) It's her. She is the screwy one. She has done something with it and forgotten. She should be put away!

MISS BLACKLOCK. You're being very rude, Mitzi. Apologize to Miss Bunner…

MITZI. No! I go! You find someone else. I not blacken your doorstep again.

*(With this **MITZI** turns and exits.)*

MISS BLACKLOCK. I do apologize for that outburst. Regrettable – but she's always like it.

CRADDOCK. I'm afraid she can't leave.

MISS BLACKLOCK. Oh, She won't, don't worry. She's such an explosive person.

BUNNY. And a *liar!* You should check up on her, Inspector. I dare say we'd all be surprised if we knew the *truth* about *her.*

(There's a moments pause.)

MISS BLACKLOCK. *(indicating the trolley)* Well, she does make excellent coffee.

BUNNY. It's the only thing she doesn't put garlic in.

MISS BLACKLOCK. Miss Marple?

MISS MARPLE. I'd love some thank you.

MISS BLACKLOCK. Inspector?

CRADDOCK. Not right now, if you don't mind. I'd like to take another look round. Perhaps you would show me the rest of the house.

MISS BLACKLOCK. Yes, of course. Bunny, you pour the coffee, would you?

BUNNY. Oh – yes.

*(**MISS BLACKLOCK** and **CRADDOCK** exit.)*

*(**BUNNY** moves to the trolley to pour out the coffee.)*

You like it black, don't you?

MISS MARPLE. No. I like it white.

BUNNY. That's right. *(She hands **MISS MARPLE** the coffee.)*

*(**MISS MARPLE** takes a "sideways" look at it and moves discreetly to the trolley to pour some milk in, and **BUNNY** pours herself a coffee.)*

I don't know how you drink it black. I like mine with lots of milk and sugar. I've always had a sweet tooth.

(They both sit down with their coffee.)

Letty was always teasing me about it when we were children, I remember.

MISS MARPLE. Not many friendships last as long as yours.

BUNNY. She rescued me, you know.

MISS MARPLE. *(puzzled)* From what?

BUNNY. I was destitute.

MISS MARPLE. Surely not.

BUNNY. Don't you believe me?

MISS MARPLE. Oh, yes – of course.

BUNNY. She's so good. Not only to me – everyone.

MISS MARPLE. She does seem to take rather a lot of people under her wing.

BUNNY. Too trusting. Too trusting by far.

MISS MARPLE. She doesn't strike me as the sort of person who's easily fooled.

BUNNY. She's not a woman of the world, you know. Not like us.

MISS MARPLE. But, if she worked for Randall Goedler all those years…

(BUNNY *almost drops her coffee, but recovers.*)

BUNNY. *(flustered)* Oh, yes. She did. Who told you that?

MISS MARPLE. You did. The other day.

BUNNY. It's a secret. Don't tell anybody. Poor Lotty. Poor, poor, Lotty. Whenever I think of her that poem comes to mind.

MISS MARPLE. What poem's that?

BUNNY. *(indignantly)* Why, the one that goes… "And sad affliction bravely borne." *(She sighs.)*

MISS MARPLE. What "sad affliction," Miss Bunner?

BUNNY. *(distantly)* I – what?

MISS MARPLE. Sad affliction.

BUNNY. All those years looking after her sister – only she would have done it.

MISS MARPLE. Tuberculosis, wasn't it?

BUNNY. Gave up everything – everything. Nobody appreciates her – not like I do. And that Patrick… He's always taking advantage of her.

MISS MARPLE. He seems such a nice young man.

BUNNY. Huh! He keeps borrowing money from her and never paying it back. It wouldn't surprise me if it was him who put that Rudi Scherz up to coming here last night. Always playing practical jokes. They were probably going to share the proceeds so he could give Letty the money he owes her. *(She quivers visibly.)* He's like all the young people these days. They've no respect – for anything.

MISS MARPLE. Things aren't all that easy for them, you know.

BUNNY. Come and look at this…

*(**BUNNY** gets up and goes to the sideboard by the wall where the bullets entered. **MISS MARPLE** is close on her heels.)*

See what one of them did to this beautiful sideboard. There. A cigarette burn. It's only the young people who smoke in this house.

MISS MARPLE. What a shame.

BUNNY. Such a beautiful piece.

MISS MARPLE. Yes, so is this. *(She indicates the Dresden figure.)*

BUNNY. Dresden. We have two. A shepherd here. And a shepherdess in the spare room.

MISS MARPLE. No. This is the shepherdess, Miss Bunner.

BUNNY. Oh! I always thought the shepherd was in this room. Oh, dear, oh dear. This dreadful business, Miss Marple. It really has got on top of me. I'm more confused than ever.

MISS MARPLE. *(noticing the dead violets)* Good gracious. I am sorry, Miss Bunner. The violets have died. I'd hoped they'd stay fresh all through next week.

BUNNY. How silly of me. I forgot to water them.

MISS MARPLE. But…

BUNNY. No wonder.

MISS MARPLE. Well, never mind. I'll bring you lots more and I think I know someone who can repair this so you'd never notice it had been damaged.

BUNNY. That would be wonderful.

MISS MARPLE. I really ought to be going now.

BUNNY. Must you? It's so nice having someone to talk to who understands.

MISS MARPLE. I have some shopping to do.

(**MISS MARPLE** *moves to the Locked Door but cannot open it.*)

BUNNY. Oh, no. That one's always sealed up. This table used to be in front of it. Then people knew they couldn't go through.

MISS MARPLE. Seems like a good idea.

BUNNY. It was. But, Phillipa suggested it would be better here. She said it would – integrate – the rooms more. It was two rooms originally, you see.

(**MISS MARPLE** *turns back to the door and looks at it more closely. She notices the hinges have been oiled.*)

MISS MARPLE. *(thoughtfully)* Is there a key?

BUNNY. Ah. The builders were very clever. You see, the same key fits all the locks on the downstairs rooms. So sensible. But there's a different key for each bedroom.

MISS MARPLE. *(wryly)* So sensible.

BUNNY. I'll show you.

(**BUNNY** *goes to the Main Door and takes the key out of the lock. She returns to the Locked Door with it and tries to unlock it. It is a little difficult and* **MISS MARPLE** *steps in to help.*)

You see – it's very stiff. But you still can't open it.

(**MISS MARPLE** *however, manages to unlock it without much trouble. It swings open in absolute silence.*)

(**MISS BLACKLOCK** *enters through the Main Door.*)

MISS BLACKLOCK. *(indignantly)* What are you doing? This door hasn't been...

MISS MARPLE. *(embarrassed)* I – I really am terribly sorry...

MISS BLACKLOCK. Miss Marple!

BUNNY. Oh, Letty – it was all my fault. I was explaining to Miss Marple about Phillipa suggesting you move the table away from the door.

MISS MARPLE. It was my fault, Miss Blacklock. I'm afraid I have an insatiable curiosity. Please don't blame Miss Bunner. *(She closes the door.)* I really am sorry.

MISS BLACKLOCK. No – there's no need. With all that's been going on I'm afraid I'm a little overwrought.

MISS MARPLE. My nerves are a little on edge too.

(MISS BLACKLOCK moves closer to the door.)

MISS BLACKLOCK. This door hasn't been opened since they'd made these two rooms into one. And I believe that was at the end of the last century.

(The Main Door opens and CRADDOCK enters, holding a coffee cup.)

CRADDOCK. Ah, Miss Bunner. My Sergeant's found your missing coffee cup. In the bushes by the duck pond.

BUNNY. How lovely. I should have asked you to find it in the first place, shouldn't I? You being a detective.

CRADDOCK. *(wryly)* Yes – it's all part of the job – we find missing budgerigars as well.

MISS BLACKLOCK. But, how did my coffee cup get there?

CRADDOCK. *(mildly sarcastic)* Using my obvious powers of detection – I would say someone threw it there. *(He smiles at MISS MARPLE, who is sharing the joke.)* Have you any idea why there should be oil in it, Miss Blacklock?

MISS MARPLE. I think I have, Inspector.

CRADDOCK. Surprise me, Miss Marple.

MISS MARPLE. The hinges have been oiled – quite recently, I'd say.

(CRADDOCK moves to the Locked Door and, after examining it, opens it during the following speech.)

CRADDOCK. What! So that it would open silently. So if Rudi Scherz had an accomplice – it could have been anyone in this room last night. Why should he need to use this door? Well whoever he is, he's the only one who knows the door can be opened, and he may try to use it again. Let's hope I'm here when he does.

(The clock chimes the half hour.)

Eleven-thirty. I must get back to the station. Would you like a lift, Miss Marple?

MISS MARPLE. Oh thank you. How very kind.

MISS BLACKLOCK. Goodness, I haven't fed the ducks yet…

BUNNY. Can I help you, Letty?

(BUNNY, CRADDOCK and MISS BLACKLOCK move to the Main Door. MISS MARPLE goes to the sofa to pick up her knitting-bag.)

MISS BLACKLOCK. Well – all right, come along, Poor creatures must be wondering what's gone wrong today. Good-bye, Miss Marple.

(CRADDOCK, MISS BLACKLOCK and BUNNY exit through the Main Door. MISS MARPLE picks up the knitting-bag and moves to the Main Door.)

MRS. SWETTENHAM. *(off, calling)* Letty. Letty.

(The Locked Door swings open and MRS. SWETTENHAM enters. She has a jar of honey. She moves downstage and stands there.)

(MISS MARPLE hears this as she is going out and closing the Main Door.)

It's me – Clara. I forgot to leave the honey…

(curtain)

ACT TWO

Scene I

(The same. The following Sunday afternoon.)

(MISS BLACKLOCK, PATRICK, BUNNY and PHILLIPA are in the drawing-room. MISS BLACKLOCK, PATRICK and PHILLIPA are sitting trying to read the Sunday newspapers, but BUNNY is sitting twiddling her thumbs, intent on getting their attention; clearly she is feeling sorry for herself.)

BUNNY. It was a lovely birthday present, Letty...

MISS BLACKLOCK. I'm sorry, Bunny. It would have been a better present if I could have got into the shops yesterday.

BUNNY. No. No. A box of handkerchiefs was just what I wanted. *(But we realize it was not.)*

PATRICK. *(a bit awkwardly)* I'll, er – get you something on Monday, Bunny.

BUNNY. I don't want you to put yourself to any trouble, Patrick.

PATRICK. If only the Inspector had let us get away earlier – I really am sorry...

MISS BLACKLOCK. So am I, Bunny – about the party as well...

PHILLIPA. But, we couldn't have gone ahead with it, could we?

BUNNY. No. That's what I said. I'll have to cancel my birthday party after this dreadful business. I don't mind – it doesn't upset me...

PATRICK. I didn't see why we couldn't have gone ahead with it. I mean, a man none of us knew – came here – tried to rob us and almost killed Aunt Letty – and just because he got what he deserved, you decide poor Bunny has to suffer.

PHILLIPA. I can't believe that even *you* can be so insensitive, Patrick.

PATRICK. Oh, I'm quite sensitive sometimes – I mean, I have noticed the way you and Edmund Swettenham look at each other.

(**PHILLIPA** *seethes, but tries to control it.*)

PHILLIPA. What's wrong, Patrick? Are you jealous?

MISS BLACKLOCK. Whatever's this? Lover's tiff?

PHILLIPA. *(too quickly on the defensive)* It most certainly isn't that!

PATRICK. *(seizing the opportunity to tease)* Careful, darling. You know what they say about the lady who doth protest too much.

(**BUNNY** *realizes she has lost her position as the centre of attraction and she cannot allow this situation to continue.*)

BUNNY. Oh dear, oh dear. Please don't argue. I have such a headache. But what with that dreadful shooting – and all those questions – well, the pain – *(she holds a hand to her head)* – is quite devastating...

MISS BLACKLOCK. *(a little irritatedly)* Why don't you take something for it?

BUNNY. No, no – I shall be all right.

MISS BLACKLOCK. Don't be silly.

BUNNY. I can't find my aspirins anywhere, Letty.

MISS BLACKLOCK. There's a bottle of aspirin on my bedside table.

BUNNY. *(weakening)* Thank you – I'm quite capable of withstanding it...

MISS BLACKLOCK. Of course you are – but, why suffer?

BUNNY. Well…

MISS BLACKLOCK. Shall I go?

BUNNY. No, no, no – the least I can do is get them myself.

(BUNNY *gets "painfully" to her feet and making a "great drama" of it exits through the Main Door.*)

PHILLIPA. *(to MISS BLACKLOCK)* You really do know her well, don't you Miss Blacklock? She surprised me this time. Holding out so long before mentioning her "headache."

PHILLIPA. But you said she'd develop a stinker – and you were right.

PATRICK. It's a pity we couldn't have the party. She's been looking forward to it so much.

MISS BLACKLOCK. I'm glad it was her suggestion to cancel it.

PATRICK. I mean – where's the harm…?

(There is a pause.)

MISS BLACKLOCK. *(to PHILLIPA, appealingly)* If we had her cake with tea – and sort of turned it into a small – party just for the family?

PATRICK. It'd cheer her up no end. Only a teeny weeny party…

PHILLIPA. Oh blast you. You're making me feel dreadful.

PATRICK. I'll buy you a milk stout down at the One Tun…

PHILLIPA. Oh, go away. Well, we've got to have tea anyway. So, why not!

MISS BLACKLOCK. Oh, good. Get Julia and tell Mitzi we're going to have the cake after all.

PATRICK. Right – oh.

*(*PATRICK *exits through the Main Door.)*

MISS BLACKLOCK. Phillipa I don't want to be inquisitive – but there's something worrying you, isn't there?

PHILLIPA. *(after a moments pause)* Well…

MISS BLACKLOCK. Is it anything to do with your son?

PHILLIPA. No, he's fine. He loves his school – the fees – well, obviously they're a bit of a problem...

MISS BLACKLOCK. Ah – then there is something...

PHILLIPA. It'll be all right...

MISS BLACKLOCK. Anything you tell me will be in the strictest confidence.

PHILLIPA. There's nothing to tell – really.

MISS BLACKLOCK. Very well. But, I've got something to tell you that may help ease your worries.

PHILLIPA. They're nothing I can't cope with.

MISS BLACKLOCK. I know you're very independent, Phillipa. I can't help you much at the moment but perhaps soon...

PHILLIPA. Please, Letty – don't give it another thought. I shall be able to manage.

MISS BLACKLOCK. I want you to know, I spoke to my solicitor yesterday. I'm changing my will. Apart from Bunny's legacy – everything goes to you.

(**PHILLIPA** *is completely taken aback.*)

PHILLIPA. Me? But you can't be serious...

MISS BLACKLOCK. Oh, yes – it's all in hand.

PHILLIPA. But, I don't want it. You mustn't do this. What about Patrick and Julia?

MISS BLACKLOCK. They have no claim on me. You are now the main beneficiary.

PHILLIPA. Why? Why are you telling me all this?

MISS BLACKLOCK. Well. I don't think it's at all a bad idea for people to know that I'm changing my will.

PHILLIPA. I can't let you do it...

MISS BLACKLOCK. Believe me, Phillipa, there's a very good reason for what I'm doing. You won't get much if I die now, but if I live, one day you'll come into a lot of money.

PHILLIPA. Die? You're not going to *die.*

MISS BLACKLOCK. You never know.

(The Main Door opens and **MITZI** *enters to announce the arrival of* **MISS MARPLE, MRS. SWETTENHAM** *and* **EDMUND SWETTENHAM** *in her usual stilted manner.)*

MITZI. Here are Miss Marple, Mrs. Swettenham and Edmund Swettenham. Thank you, you're welcome.

*(***MITZI*** *exits* **MISS BLACKLOCK** *gets up to greet the arrivals, who all have little packages.)*

MISS BLACKLOCK. Miss Marple, Clara. This *is* a surprise… *(Breaking off.)*
There's nothing wrong, is there?

MRS. SWETTENHAM. Wrong?

MISS MARPLE. *(laughingly)* I suppose when the three of us turn up here these days *it does* seem as *if* trouble isn't far behind!

MRS. SWETTENHAM. *(indignantly)* Well, I certainly hope it is! I've had enough for one weekend!

MISS MARPLE. It's all my fault. Dropping in like this. I called round to Clara and Edmund to suggest it – hope you don't mind. It seemed such a shame. Miss Bunner having to cancel her party.

MRS. SWETTENHAM. We thought we'd bring her a little present each. I'm afraid we haven't got anything very exciting.

MISS BLACKLOCK. But how kind.

MRS. SWETTENHAM. We won't stay, of course.

MISS BLACKLOCK. Oh, but you must stay to tea. Mitzi's made a beautiful cake – and Bunny will be so pleased.

MISS MARPLE. We'd love to stay. Thank you.

(The **SWETTENHAMS** *and* **MISS MARPLE** *look at one another questioningly.* **EDMUND** *ventures first.)*

EDMUND. Yes. Is that all right with you, Phillipa?

PHILLIPA. *(surprised)* Oh – well – yes, of course…

MISS BLACKLOCK. Good.

*(***JULIA** *and* **PATRICK** *enter through the Main Door.)*

JULIA. Well. It looks as if we're going to have a party after all.

MISS BLACKLOCK. Well, we won't have the party – just tea.

MRS. SWETTENHAM. By the way, Letty. Did you find the honey?

MISS BLACKLOCK. Oh, Clara. I am sorry. I forgot. Thank you very much.

MRS. SWETTENHAM. I came in the back door and couldn't find you anywhere. How silly of me forgetting to leave it in the first place. We got all the way home before we noticed, didn't we, Edmund?

EDMUND. *(long sufferingly)* I'm sure we could have left it until some other time.

MRS. SWETTENHAM. But, it was your idea...

(A moment's pause.)

MISS BLACKLOCK. Actually we did need it. Mitzi always uses honey in her special cake.

MRS. SWETTENHAM. *(to* EDMUND*)* You see.

*(*EDMUND *ignores her and turns to* MISS MARPLE.*)*

EDMUND. Well, Miss Marple, looks like this time you'll be in at the kill.

(There is a pause. His tactless attitude is not appreciated.)

MRS. SWETTENHAM. Don't say things like that, Edmund. That's something we all want to forget.

EDMUND. How can we. It's by no means over.

PHILLIPA. I'm afraid you're right, Edmund.

MRS. SWETTENHAM. *(worried)* I'm sure the Inspector is satisfied...

JULIA. I don't think he is.

PATRICK. He thinks someone paid Rudi Scherz to kill Aunt Letty – and they'll try again.

MISS BLACKLOCK. You shouldn't have mentioned that, Patrick.

EDMUND. Good God. That puts all of us under suspicion.

MISS MARPLE. I'm afraid Inspector Craddock has to include all of us here now.

PATRICK. Yes. How long were you out in the hall, Miss Marple? We only have your word for it that you were coming up the drive when the shots were fired.

*(A moment's pause. All eyes are on **MISS MARPLE**.)*

MISS MARPLE. My dear boy. I'm sure *I'm very* high on his list.

PHILLIPA. Really? *(In a snide voice.)* And you seem to get on so well with him.

MISS MARPLE. I think he finds me mildly amusing...

MISS BLACKLOCK. *(after a pause, changing the subject)* Patrick, why don't you see if Bunny's coming.

*(**PATRICK** goes to the Main Door and opens it a chink to look through.)*

MRS. SWETTENHAM. Surely there's not going to be any more... unpleasantness?

EDMUND. By that d'you mean any more *murders,* Mother.

MRS. SWETTENHAM. Do you have to?

MISS BLACKLOCK. Well, I think that it's all over, too. So, let's forget it, shall we? And try to enjoy ourselves.

*(**PATRICK** closes the door.)*

PATRICK. She's coming. *(He returns to the others.)*

*(After a moment of waiting, the Main Door opens and **BUNNY** enters. She has the bottle of aspirin in her hand, and is surprised to see them all.)*

ALL. Happy Birthday, Bunny.

*(**BUNNY** beams like a child, as she goes to them.)*

BUNNY. But, I cancelled my party.

MISS BLACKLOCK. We're all going to have some cake and a cup of tea, Bunny.

BUNNY. Oh, what a lovely surprise.

*(**MISS MARPLE** hands **BUNNY** a small parcel.)*

MISS MARPLE. And here's a little something to wish you a very happy birthday, Miss Bunner.

BUNNY. *(taking it)* Thank you. That is kind. Miss Marple I'm afraid it's only handkerchiefs.

*(**BUNNY**'s face drops.)*

BUNNY. *(bravely)* Just what I wanted…

*(**EDMUND** hands her a bag.)*

EDMUND. *(apologetically)* It's only apples from the garden…

*(**BUNNY**'s face drops even more.)*

BUNNY. What a lovely thought…

*(**MRS. SWETTENHAM** hands her a wrapped jar of honey.)*

MRS. SWETTENHAM. And I've brought you some honey…

BUNNY. How kind.

MRS. SWETTENHAM. I'm afraid but the bees aren't so very busy just now, so it's only half a jar…

BUNNY. Oh, well – it can't be helped. *(pause)* I must take these aspirin. I have a thumping headache still…

MISS BLACKLOCK. Patrick. There's some soda water on the sideboard.

BUNNY. Aren't I silly having a headache on my birthday.

*(**PATRICK** goes to the sideboard, takes out a glass and squirts soda into it, then gives the glass to **BUNNY** and replaces the soda water. **BUNNY** takes the glass from him, pops a couple of aspirin in her mouth and swallows them with the aid of the soda water. There is a moment's pause – as all eyes are on her)*

MISS BLACKLOCK. You'll soon feel better.

*(The Main Door opens and **MITZI** enters pushing the trolley. On it is an enormous chocolate cake – Delicious Death. It has one enormous candle in the middle. Ideally, the candle should be lit.)*

*(Everyone turns as **MITZI** pushes the trolley across the room.)*

MISS MARPLE. What a magnificent cake.

MITZI. I excel myself. This time I put a special *secret* ingredient in. Give it that extra bit of *flavour.* Make it *more* than perfect.

PHILLIPA. Have you noticed the candle, Bunny.

BUNNY. Yes.

PATRICK. Only *one?*

MISS MARPLE. Of course. There isn't room for all *twenty-one* candles, is there?

MISS BLACKLOCK. *(smiling)* You've got to blow out the candle, Bunny.

*(**BUNNY** steps forward – a picture of happiness. She huffs and puffs before the candle flickers and goes out. They give her a cheer.)*

PHILLIPA. Do hurry up and cut it, Bunny.

JULIA. Yes, we're all *dying* to try it.

*(They watch as **BUNNY** picks up the knife and cuts the first piece of cake. She places it on one of the small plates there and offers it.)*

BUNNY. Who's first?

MISS MARPLE. You! You're the birthday person. You must eat the first slice.

JULIA. Go on, Bunny. I'll cut the rest.

*(**JULIA** moves to start cutting the cake into pieces. **BUNNY** starts to nibble on the cake.)*

MISS BLACKLOCK. Don't forget to make a wish.

*(**BUNNY** takes a huge bite and closes her eyes to make a wish. **JULIA** starts to hand the cake around. Everyone takes a piece but does not actually start eating it yet. They are still watching **BUNNY**, who is still wishing.)*

PATRICK. What are you wishing, Bunny?

*(**BUNNY** opens her eyes and smiles at him.)*

BUNNY. I'm not telling. It won't come true.

JULIA. If I were you, I'd wish him dead.

PATRICK. If you weren't my sister...

JULIA. *(with an insincere smile)* But I am...

> *(Suddenly,* **BUNNY** *starts coughing. It gets worse and becomes a choking noise.)*

MRS. SWETTENHAM. Someone bang her back.

> *(Before anyone can do this* **BUNNY** *gives a final choke – cheeks puffing and eyes bulging – and drops to the floor. There is a moment, as they all stand there, immobilized; shock and horror beginning to dig into them. Then* **MISS BLACKLOCK** *moves to* **BUNNY** *and the others gather round)*

MISS BLACKLOCK. *(kneeling)* It's the excitement – it's been too much for her... *(She undoes the neck of* **BUNNY***'s blouse.)*

> *(***MISS MARPLE** *joins* **MISS BLACKLOCK** *on her knees so that* **BUNNY** *is between them.)*

MISS BLACKLOCK. Someone get some brandy...

PHILLIPA. Surely we should call the doctor.

JULIA. I'll call him. Letty, what's the doctor's number?

MISS BLACKLOCK. Five-eight.

> *(***JULIA** *is about to telephone this when* **MISS MARPLE** *stops her.)*

MISS MARPLE. *(quickly)* I'm afraid there's no need...

> *(All eyes turn to* **MISS MARPLE.***)*

It's too late.

> *(***PATRICK,** *who has been hovering with his piece of cake, looks down at the plate in his hands)*

PATRICK. Delicious Death!

> *(curtain)*

Scene II

(The same. The following Monday morning.)

*(As the curtain rises, **PATRICK** and **JULIA** are alone in the room.)*

JULIA. What are we going to do?

PATRICK. We'll think of something...

JULIA. They're bound to find out – it can't last much longer...

PATRICK. Don't worry...

JULIA. Don't worry? For God's sake, Patrick!

PATRICK. We'll achieve nothing by panicking.

JULIA. You will help me, won't you?

PATRICK. Haven't I – I've done everything you've asked...

JULIA. I know – you've been wonderful.

(They kiss.)

I need you.

PATRICK. Well, there's no way back. Can't stop now.

JULIA. What's done is done.

PATRICK. I did it for you...

(They kiss momentarily, then break quickly.)

*(The Main Door opens and **MISS BLACKLOCK** and **INSPECTOR CRADDOCK** enter. She looks worn and tired. Clearly, she feels the loss of **BUNNY** deeply.)*

CRADDOCK. Ah. Good morning, Miss Simmons. How are you, Mr. Simmons?

PATRICK. *(warily)* Well – thank you.

JULIA. Have you found out any more?

CRADDOCK. We're making progress – we're not interrupting anything, are we?

PATRICK. *(a shade too quickly)* Oh, no – nothing at all.

JULIA. No...

CRADDOCK. Well...

PATRICK. Oh, I see. We'll go and feed the ducks or something.

*(**PATRICK** and **JULIA** are about to exit.)*

CRADDOCK. Mr. Simmons…

*(**PATRICK** and **JULIA** stop and **PATRICK** turns to **CRADDOCK**. They are quite close.)*

PATRICK. *(nervously)* Yes?

CRADDOCK. Did you know you've got lipstick on your collar?

*(**PATRICK**'s hand shoots up to his shirt collar. Clearly, he is embarrassed, and **JULIA** is, too. But she makes a better job of hiding her embarrassment)*

PATRICK. I – didn't – I mean – I didn't put a clean shirt on this morning…

CRADDOCK. Well, he can't blame you, can he Miss Simmons?

JULIA. Hardly.

PATRICK. Well – the ducks…

(They are about to move off.)

CRADDOCK. By the way, Miss Simmons?

JULIA. Yes?

CRADDOCK. You work in the pharmacy at the local hospital, don't you?

JULIA. *(warily)* That's right.

CRADDOCK. Thank you.

*(**PATRICK** and **JULIA** continue on their way to the Main Door and exit without another word.)*

There are more urgent things. Now, Miss Blacklock.

MISS BLACKLOCK. I'm really not up to answering a lot of questions.

CRADDOCK. *(sympathetically)* I'll be as brief as I can. But, you've had another lucky escape.

MISS BLACKLOCK. I find it more and more difficult to accept your reasoning, Inspector. How can you possibly suggest that I was the intended victim this time? Any one of us could have eaten that cake first.

CRADDOCK. I know that...

MISS BLACKLOCK. And Patrick's suggestion that Clara's honey could have been poisoned is – it's malicious!

CRADDOCK. I agree.

MISS BLACKLOCK. *(in surprise)* Oh? Then how was the cake poisoned? Did Mitzi–

CRADDOCK. *(interrupting)* It wasn't the cake –

MISS BLACKLOCK. But...

(She breaks off, clearly upset. He takes out a bottle of aspirin.)

CRADDOCK. – it was these.

(She looks at the bottle of aspirin, amazed.)

MISS BLACKLOCK. My aspirin?

CRADDOCK. Exactly. *Your* aspirin. The ones you normally keep by your bed.

MISS BLACKLOCK. *(painfully)* No – no...

CRADDOCK. Someone wants you dead – very, very badly!

(A moment's pause. The tension builds.)

MISS BLACKLOCK. I – I'm frightened, Inspector.

CRADDOCK. At last! Now perhaps you'll help me find the murderer.

MISS BLACKLOCK. *(sharply)* I haven't purposely been non-cooperative. I just couldn't believe anyone would... *(She breaks off.)*

CRADDOCK. There's no friendship where money's concerned. Did you know Belle Goedler's condition has deteriorated recently?

MISS BLACKLOCK. I knew she wasn't well...

CRADDOCK. I understand from the Scottish police that she's now seriously *ill.*

MISS BLACKLOCK. I should go to her. Poor Belle…

CRADDOCK. It could be poor Miss Blacklock.

(She looks at him, afraid.)

MISS BLACKLOCK. Pip and Emma…

CRADDOCK. Yes. They are uppermost in my mind, but it could be a combination of them and their parents who are trying to kill you. The father. Dimitri Stanfordis. You said he was a rogue. Would he go as far as murder to *get* money?

(A moment's pause.)

MISS BLACKLOCK. *(fearfully)* I'll do anything you say.

CRADDOCK. Good. You must try to remember everything you can about him – Sonia – and Pip and Emma. Anything and everything. But, the son and daughter in particular. They're uppermost in my mind. Have you any photographs of them?

MISS BLACKLOCK. Well – Belle Goedler is more likely to have photographs of them than I am.

CRADDOCK. I'm afraid we drew almost a complete blank with her. They allowed the police up there to look all over the house – they found nothing. Have you anything? What I'm hoping is that Pip may take after his father – or Emma her mother…

MISS BLACKLOCK. Or the other way round…

CRADDOCK. Exactly.

MISS BLACKLOCK. There was an old album. I haven't seen it for years. It should be in the house somewhere…

CRADDOCK. Find it!

MISS BLACKLOCK. It might take a little while.

CRADDOCK. Would you like some help?

MISS BLACKLOCK. Let me try first! *(MISS BLACKLOCK opens the Main Door.)*

(PHILLIPA is standing there. She enters. MISS BLACKLOCK waits a moment, then exits, closing the door behind her.)

PHILLIPA. I believe you want to see me?

CRADDOCK. Yes, Mrs. Haymes. Do sit down.

(PHILLIPA *sits rather hesitantly.*)

PHILLIPA. Oh, dear – this sounds serious.

CRADDOCK. *(after a pause)* If you lie about something, Mrs. Haymes – you have to cover your tracks very, very carefully.

PHILLIPA. I – I don't...

CRADDOCK. Yes, you do understand. Don't lie any more. You know what I'm talking about.

(*A moment's pause. During this and the following,* PHILLIPA *clenches and unclenches her hands.*)

PHILLIPA. *(bitterly)* Everyone says we have more freedom nowadays – the world is – more understanding – than it ever was. Well, Inspector Craddock, you try being an unmarried mother...

CRADDOCK. I don't think it would work!

(*She smiles in spite of herself.*)

PHILLIPA. It isn't easy in a small village.

CRADDOCK. So, you invented a husband!

PHILLIPA. How do you think Letty Blacklock would react if she Knew the truth?

CRADDOCK. She strikes me as being a sympathetic and understanding person. What's more, she's no fool. I've a sneaking suspicion she may have guessed the truth.

(PHILLIPA*'s hand goes up to her mouth.*)

PHILLIPA. So, that's why...

CRADDOCK. What?

PHILLIPA. She's so kind to me – there aren't many like her.

CRADDOCK. Does your son know the truth?

PHILLIPA. He believes – his father died...

CRADDOCK. Silly. He'll find out sometime.

PHILLIPA. Maybe.

CRADDOCK. My advice to you is to tell him – and everyone else.

PHILLIPA. Will you tell the others if I don't? It isn't a crime.

CRADDOCK. I couldn't live with it. But, it's up to you.

PHILLIPA. How did you find out.

CRADDOCK. We do a lot of routine work.

PHILLIPA. You've been checking up on me?

CRADDOCK. Sort of.

PHILLIPA. You make it sound very casual.

CRADDOCK. It isn't, But it *is puzzling.*

(*A moment's pause.*)

PHILLIPA. Puzzling?

CRADDOCK. It's only a small thing – but I'm sure you can help. It's about your son's birth certificate.

PHILLIPA. (*warily*) Yes?

CRADDOCK. It gives the mother's name as – Phillipa Haymes.

PHILLIPA. (*nervously*) Well – that's me.

CRADDOCK. Ah, well – in that case, there is a problem.

(**PHILLIPA** *drops her head.*)

You see – we can't find a birth certificate – for anyone with your name – well, not one that corresponds with what we know about you.

(**PHILLIPA** *looks up at him and bites her lip.*)

(*The Main Door opens and* **MISS BLACKLOCK** *enters, carrying a photographic album.*)

MISS BLACKLOCK. I've found it… Am I interrupting?

CRADDOCK. Your timing is perfect. Mrs. Haymes and I have just finished. (*He pauses.*) For the time being!

(**PHILLIPA** *gets up, her mind cleanly in a whirl, and exits without a word. Closing the door behind her.*)

Are there any photos of Sonia and her husband?

MISS BLACKLOCK. I haven't had a chance to look yet.

(**CRADDOCK** *starts to turn the pages of the album.*)

CRADDOCK. *(pointing)* Is that her?

MISS BLACKLOCK. No – that's Belle. Isn't she beautiful?

CRADDOCK. *(reading)* "Belle at Skeyne?"

MISS BLACKLOCK. That's their place in Scotland. I'm afraid the writing is rather faded.

CRADDOCK. Tell me when there's one of Sonia and Dimitri. *(He continues to turn the pages and then stops abruptly. He then holds up the album so that we can see two facing pages that are blank. He peers closely at the blank pages. Reading).* "Sonia and Dimitri – Dimitri – Belle, Dimitri and Sonia – Skeyne. Belle, Self and Sonia." *(He stops reading.)* Someone got to this ahead of you, Miss Blacklock, didn't they?

MISS BLACKLOCK. It looks as though they've been ripped out.

(He flicks over a few more pages and then stops, holding up what are clearly some old letters.)

CRADDOCK. Letters.

MISS BLACKLOCK. They'll be from me to my sister. *(She holds out her hand to take them.)*

CRADDOCK. If you've no objection I'd like to skim through these.

MISS BLACKLOCK. Well…

CRADDOCK. *(refusing to be put off)* There might be something – about – Sonia – or Dimitri.

*(As **CRADDOCK** mentions the name the Main Door opens and **MITZI** enters, with outdoor clothes on, and carrying a suitcase.)*

MITZI. Miss Blacklock…

MISS BLACKLOCK. *(irritatedly)* Please, Mitzi. Not now. I don't want to be interrupted at the moment.

MITZI. I not interrupt! I give you the sack! I go! *(She turns and makes her way back to the Main Door.)*

MISS BLACKLOCK. Mitzi…

(MITZI *does not answer. She exits without a backward glance, slamming the door behind her.*)

(MISS BLACKLOCK *turns to* CRADDOCK.)

(appealing) She can't go…

CRADDOCK. Certainly not.

MISS BLACKLOCK. I'll go after her.

CRADDOCK. Of course. And when you catch up with her, you might tell her that she won't get any further than the bus station.

(MISS BLACKLOCK *makes a hurried exit.*)

(CRADDOCK *sits down and starts to read the letters.*)

(*After a moment the Main Door opens and* MISS MARPLE *enters.*)

MISS MARPLE. Inspector!

CRADDOCK. *(covering the letters)* Ah, my little sleuth. You're just in time.

MISS MARPLE. Some people say I'm like a bad penny.

CRADDOCK. But, not me, Miss Marple – not me.

MISS MARPLE. I passed Miss Blacklock – she told me to come in. That girl of hers, Mitzi, was haring down the drive like a maniac.

CRADDOCK. She is rather peculiar, isn't she? Well. Now you're here you can make yourself useful and help me with a little research. *(He holds up a letter.)*

MISS MARPLE. Certainly, but I do have to talk to Miss Blacklock…

CRADDOCK. It won't take long – and I don't think you'd want to pass up the opportunity of going through someone's old letters!

MISS MARPLE. *(with a broad smile)* Inspector! That's not like me – whose are they!

(CRADDOCK *holds the letters out to her. She takes them.*)

CRADDOCK. It's from Miss Blacklock to her sister, Charlotte. If you find anything that might be helpful – *as well as interesting* – read it out to me, please.

MISS MARPLE. Very well.

(They sit down opposite each other and start reading.)

CRADDOCK. Here's something that's been mentioned before.

MISS MARPLE. Oh?

CRADDOCK. It refers to her disfigurement – Charlotte's that is. *(Reading.)* "It's not as bad as you think it is and you shouldn't lock yourself away... "

MISS MARPLE. I wonder what it was – this disfigurement?

CRADDOCK. It doesn't say specifically – I don't suppose it was anything much...

MISS MARPLE. Then why should she lock herself away?

CRADDOCK. In my experience, most women are extremely vain. How would you react if you had a mole on the end of your nose?

MISS MARPLE. I wouldn't have to look at it.

CRADDOCK. But, most women would hide themselves behind a veil.

(They go back to their respective letters.)

MISS MARPLE. It's mentioned in this one, too. Listen. *(Reading.)* "I do wish you'd get out more. No one else notices it."

CRADDOCK. You see. Pure vanity! Miss Marple. *(Thoughtfully.)* Maybe.

CRADDOCK. *(still looking at his letter)* Ah. This is what I've been looking for.

MISS MARPLE. What is it?

CRADDOCK. About Sonia Goedler – the fights she had with her brother. *(Reading.)* "Sonia has such a violent temper. It's quite terrifying sometimes."

MISS MARPLE. Did you ever find any photographs of Sonia?

CRADDOCK. They've disappeared – rather conveniently. But, violent temper, and Miss Blacklock says she was dark and attractive. Makes you think, doesn't it?

MISS MARPLE. *(thoughtfully)* Yes. It does indeed Inspector. *(She goes back to her letter.)* Here's something interesting. *(reading)* "You can always tell when Sonia is angry. She has the habit of clenching and unclenching her hands." Who does that remind you of?

CRADDOCK. You've got me there. That's something I've missed.

MISS MARPLE. And, you don't miss much, do you? Julia Simmons does it when she's – agitated. I've been keeping a very careful watch on that young woman.

CRADDOCK. Well, I've checked out both Julia and Patrick Simmons. The French police contacted their mother in the South of France and she confirmed that they were staying here.

MISS MARPLE. Really? There's no mistake?

CRADDOCK. Well, unless the woman in the South of France *isn't* their mother.

MISS MARPLE. Could she be Sonia? Keeping out of the way until it's all over.

CRADDOCK. The French police must have checked on her. They're very thorough.

MISS MARPLE. So, she is Letty Blacklock's cousin?

CRADDOCK. Almost certainly.

MISS MARPLE. I was hoping we'd found Emma – but, I know there was always a possibility I was wrong suspecting Julia. She isn't the only one who does that hand-clenching business. Phillipa Haymes docs it as well.

CRADDOCK. That's very observant of you, Miss Marple. Ten out of ten.

MISS MARPLE. It's very frustrating that there isn't a photograph of Sonia.

CRADDOCK. Yes. Sonia Goedler seems to have disappeared off the face of the earth.

MISS MARPLE. I wonder what this means? *(Reading.)* "Lots of love, darling, and buck up. This iodine treatment may make a lot of difference."

CRADDOCK. *(thoughtfully)* It must have been some special kind of treatment they used in those days.

MISS MARPLE. For what?

CRADDOCK. TB. That is why Miss Blacklock sent her sister to Switzerland.

(MISS MARPLE muses. CRADDOCK moves to the album on the table and starts to flip through. Then he taps the album with his finger.)

Who does that remind you of?

MISS MARPLE. I must admit, it does look like Clara Swettenham but...

CRADDOCK. But what?

MISS MARPLE. Well, it is an old photograph, Inspector.

(The main door opens and MISS BLACKLOCK enters.)

MISS BLACKLOCK. I'm sorry to keep you waiting, Miss Marple. You wanted to see me?

MISS MARPLE. Yes, please. About the funeral service.

CRADDOCK. Well, I must get back to the station. I'll take these with me if you don't mind, Miss Blacklock. I'll return them later. Good bye, ladies.

(CRADDOCK exits.)

MISS MARPLE. *(as he goes)* Good bye, Inspector. *(to MISS BLACKLOCK.)* I am sorry to disturb you at a time like this. My nephew wanted you to know that he's finalized all the arrangements for the service, but he'd like to know which hymns you'd like.

MISS BLACKLOCK. "Lead Kindly Light" was her favourite hymn. Please thank him for me... *(She breaks off, grief-stricken.)*

(MISS MARPLE is unable to do or say anything for a moment. Then with a supreme effort, MISS BLACKLOCK pulls herself together.)

I'm sorry – very sorry – forgive me.

MISS MARPLE. Don't. Please don't.

MISS BLACKLOCK. It came over me – suddenly – what I've lost. She was my only link with the past. The only one who – remembered. Now she's gone – I'm quite alone – quite alone…

MISS MARPLE. I understand. Cousins – nephews – nieces – are all very well. But when the last person you shared your youth with has gone – then you really are *alone*.

(*The Main Door opens and* **PHILLIPA** *enters with the morning mail.*)

PHILLIPA. Oh. I'm so sorry.

MISS MARPLE. I'm just leaving.

PHILLIPA. Not on my account, I hope?

MISS MARPLE. No, my dear. There's something I must do. Good bye, Miss Blacklock.

(**MISS BLACKLOCK.** *is now completely composed.*)

MISS BLACKLOCK. Good-bye, and thank you…

(**MISS MARPLE** *exits through the Main Door.*)

(**PHILLIPA** *hands* **MISS BLACKLOCK** *a letter.*)

PHILLIPA. Only me and you this morning. Mine's from Harry. He's looking forward to half-term.

MISS BLACKLOCK. It seems as though he's only just gone back to school…

PHILLIPA. Letty, I – realize it probably isn't the ideal time to mention it, but it is all right, isn't it? Harry coming here for half-term?

(**MISS BLACKLOCK** *opens her letter and starts to read. As she does so, the change in her expression is dramatic. From a drained look of weariness to cold, hard anger.*)

MISS BLACKLOCK. Phillipa!

(**PHILLIPA** *looks up, noticing the change.*)

PHILLIPA. What's wrong?

MISS BLACKLOCK. Where are Patrick and Julia?

PHILLIPA. I – I think they're upstairs. Why?

> (**MISS BLACKLOCK** *hands* **PHILLIPA** *the letter to read.* **PHILLIPA** *skims through it.*)

I don't understand.

MISS BLACKLOCK. *(seething)* Will you please get them for me.

> (**PHILLIPA** *nods, hands the letter back and exits through the Main Door, leaving it slightly open.*)

PHILLIPA. *(off)* Julia? Patrick? Letty wants a word with you…

> (*We hear a muffled reply. Then* **PHILLIPA** *pops her head round the door.*)

Shall I go?

MISS BLACKLOCK. I'd like you to stay.

> (**PHILLIPA** *pauses for a moment, then Liters, reluctantly.* **MISS BLACKLOCK** *is still seething.*)

> (**PATRICK** *enters alone.*)

PATRICK. Julia won't be a moment.

> (**MISS BLACKLOCK** *indicates a chair.*)

MISS BLACKLOCK. *(sharply)* Sit down!

> (**PATRICK** *is instantly aware that something is wrong.*)

PATRICK. What is it?

MISS BLACKLOCK. I've received this letter. *(Reading.)* "Dear Aunt Letty. I hope it will be all right for me to come to you on Tuesday? Patrick was going to let me know but he hasn't. My train arrives at about six-fifteen… " *(She stops reading.)* It's signed. "Yours affectionately, Julia."

PATRICK. Oh, God…

MISS BLACKLOCK. *(indicating the letter)* This is from your sister?

PATRICK. I'm afraid so.

MISS BLACKLOCK. Then who is the young woman upstairs?

PATRICK. I can explain…

MISS BLACKLOCK. Do!

PATRICK. I know it was a stupid thing to do. But, Julia – my *real* sister – didn't want to take up the job at the hospital here. You see, she was offered a job up in the North at some theatre – as an assistant stage manager. She's always been stage-struck and she knew Mother would be furious if she took it…

MISS BLACKLOCK. Will you please explain who that woman is upstairs?

PATRICK. I'm trying to. We didn't come straight here when we first came back to England. There were friends to see – parties to go to. That's how we met Juli – the one upstairs, I mean. She and I rather fell for each other and as she wasn't doing anything in particular, it seemed like a marvellous idea for the girls to swap identities. I liked it for obvious reasons. And if Mother believed my sister was here – well, she couldn't object. I was going to tell you but I couldn't in these circumstances.

MISS BLACKLOCK. Who is that young woman?

PATRICK. Well…

(*The Main Door opens and* **JULIA** *enters.*)

(**MISS BLACKLOCK** *turns to face her.*)

MISS BLACKLOCK. Who are you?

(**JULIA** *looks at* **PATRICK**. *There is a moment's pause.*)

WHO ARE YOU?

JULIA. I'm Emma Stamfordis.

(*curtain*)

Scene III

(The same. About six P.M., the same day)

*(***CRADDOCK*** *is with the "family" group –* **JULIA,
MISS BLACKLOCK, PHILLIPA** *and* **PATRICK. JULIA**
is sitting directly opposite **CRADDOCK,** *who is making
copious notes. The others are seated around.)*

CRADDOCK. I'm surprised you decided to stay, Miss
Stamfordis.

JULIA. If I'd tried to make a run for it, you'd only have
caught up with me.

CRADDOCK. You wouldn't have got out of Chipping
Cleghorn.

JULIA. Are you going to arrest me?

CRADDOCK. I would like to know where your brother is
first.

JULIA. I haven't the faintest idea.

CRADDOCK. If this is misguided family loyalty...

JULIA. I *honestly* don't know.

MISS BLACKLOCK. *Honestly.* I imagine that's a word which
doesn't come easily to you.

JULIA. I know how you must feel about me, but...

CRADDOCK. *(a tinge angrily)* Perlease. Your *brother,* Miss
Stamfordis.

JULIA. I haven't seen him since we were three years old.
When my parents split up it was agreed that I should
go with my father and Pip with my mother.

CRADDOCK. Let's try something different. Where is your
father?

JULIA. Try the moon! When I was just about old enough to
take care of myself – he left me in Istanbul. I worked
my way back here.

CRADDOCK. Where is your mother, then?

JULIA. Believe me, I'd love to know that. I've searched everywhere. She made a good job of disappearing. I even went to Scotland to see if I could get some information.

MISS BLACKLOCK. You went to see Belle?

JULIA. Why not? She's my aunt. I also hoped she might help me. But, it was no use. She's not part of this world anymore. Then I got to thinking about my uncle – of course, I knew he was very rich. It occurred to me that if Aunt Belle died, I was probably his only surviving relative. So, I went along to Somerset House and looked up his will. Was I surprised! I searched everywhere for someone who even knew Letty Blacklock. Then I had the most incredible stroke of luck. Through an acquaintance I managed to meet Patrick and his sister. When the swap was suggested I had to stop myself sounding too eager.

MISS BLACKLOCK. I admire your self-control. It must have been quite an effort waiting for the right opportunity to take a pot-shot at me.

(*The telephone rings.* MISS BLACKLOCK *answers it.*)

Hello, Chipping Cleghorn eight-seven… Hold on. Inspector, it's for you.

CRADDOCK. (*into the telephone*) Hello. Craddock here… Yes… What… Well, keep me informed. (*He replaces the receiver.*) That's a disturbing development. Miss Marple has been missing since she left here this morning.

(*A general chorus of exclamations:* "Oh, no.," "How terrible.," *etc.*)

(*Checking his watch.*) That's nearly seven hours.

(*The Main Door opens and* MITZI *enters with* MRS. SWETTENHAM *and* EDMUND.)

MITZI. (*unnaturally*) Mrs. Swettenham and her son Edmund. Thank you. You're welcome.

(JULIA *has to stifle a laugh.*)

MRS. SWETTENHAM. What is it now, Inspector?

CRADDOCK. All in good time.

MRS. SWETTENHAM. Well, I don't like policemen turning up on my doorstep and asking me to accompany them. My neighbours will be tittle-tattling for weeks.

EDMUND. I shall be writing to the newspapers about this.

CRADDOCK. That'll keep you busy for a change, won't it? (*He turns to* **MITZI.**) Now, Mitzi. You have something to tell us.

MISS BLACKLOCK. Mitzi?

MITZI. Yes. I will tell the whole truth and nothing but the truth. When I first saw what happen on Friday I not do that.

JULIA. Huh! We all know what a little liar she is!

CRADDOCK. *Per-lease!*

MITZI. I am in the dining-room. Like I say. When I hear the gun go off. I look through the keyhole and in the little moonlight – I could see – I could see Miss Blacklock (*She points at* **MISS BLACKLOCK.**)

MISS BLACKLOCK. Me? Oh Mitzi…

EDMUND. That's absurd, she couldn't possibly have seen Miss Blacklock…

CRADDOCK. Go on, Mr. Swettenham. Why stop now? Why? Why couldn't she have seen Miss Blacklock? It was because she saw *you*, wasn't it?

MRS. SWETTENHAM. Edmund – that's not possible.

CRADDOCK. If Miss Blacklock dies before Belle Goedler two people stand to benefit. Emma Stamfordis…

EDMUND. And you think I'm Pip? That's too fantastic for words.

CRADDOCK. Who told you about Pip, Mr. Swettenham? I certainly haven't and neither has anyone else in this room.

PHILLIPA. You're wrong, Inspector. I've told him…

(They all turn to look at her.)

He isn't Pip! I am.

(A moment.)

You wrongly assumed Pip was a boy. *(To* JULIA.*)* Emma, you knew the truth. Why didn't you say so?

JULIA. Because I suspected who you were. The Inspector was right. I was holding back out of family loyalty. I didn't want to give you away.

MISS BLACKLOCK. *(angrily)* You of all people, Phillipa.

PHILLIPA. *(coolly, in control)* I am sorry, Letty. But when my mother died I was desperate for money. Hers had gone years ago. She told me about the will and I discovered for myself that Belle Goedler was seriously ill.

CRADDOCK. You *had* gone to a lot of trouble.

PHILLIPA. It was important to me. I wanted security. Not for me, for my son, So, I came here.

MISS BLACKLOCK. I was prepared to help both of you.

PHILLIPA. Yes, well – it was part of my plan to get into your good books.

MISS BLACKLOCK. *(bitterly)* And it worked, didn't it?

PHILLIPA. But, I grew fond of you.

MISS BLACKLOCK. I even changed my will in your favour.

PHILLIPA. That scared me stiff. You said there was a very good reason for doing it. I thought you'd found out who I really was. That you were warning me off from trying to get my uncle's money.

MISS BLACKLOCK. *(shaking her head)* You were coming to kill me for it.

PHILLIPA. *(after a moment's pause)* It never occurred to me – even though I felt I was more entitled to it than you. But, there it is. I am Pip. And I'm glad you know. *(She turns her attention to* CRADDOCK.*)*

CRADDOCK. You two have been seeing quite a lot of each other, haven't you?

PHILLIPA. Yes. Well, there's no need to suspect Edmund any more, Inspector.

CRADDOCK. Isn't there? Mr. Swettenham's a struggling young writer – not yet published – who would very much like to marry a rich woman.

EDMUND. It's not *true!*

CRADDOCK. You're in debt up to your eyeballs.

EDMUND. Nonsense!

CRADDOCK. And I can prove it. The bank – the bookmaker...

EDMUND. So what! Does that...

MRS. SWETTENHAM. *(astonished)* It can't be right – not Edmund...

CRADDOCK. A rich wife would have solved all your problems wouldn't it? But in order for her to be rich, Miss Blacklock had to die first and you did something about that.

MRS. SWETTENHAM. Oh Edmund, no – you couldn't...

CRADDOCK. Shall we start with your meeting Rudi Scherz in Turin, Mr. Swettenham!

(**EDMUND** *exits quickly through the Main Door.*)

PHILLIPA. Wait!

MRS. SWETTENHAM. Edmund...

PATRICK. Inspector, aren't you...

CRADDOCK. He won't get far. You'll need to see your solicitor as soon as possible, Mrs. Swettenham. I'm sorry about this. I realize it must be a great shock.

MISS BLACKLOCK. It seems like a bad dream...

CRADDOCK. *(to JULIA)* I'd like to see you down at the station.

JULIA. Now?

CRADDOCK. It won't take long.

(**JULIA** *exits through the Main Door.*)

Mr. Simmons, would you take Mrs. Swettenham home, please? Patrick. Yes. Yes, of course.

CRADDOCK. A call to her doctor wouldn't do any harm.

PATRICK. *(gently)* Come along, Mrs. Swettenham... *(He takes her arm.)* It'll be all right – you see...

CRADDOCK. Mitzi, you are a magnificent liar.

MITZI. I do well. Yes. I did what you ask?

CRADDOCK. To the letter! *(To* MISS BLACKLOCK.*)* Sorry to have given you such a fright.

MISS BLACKLOCK. You *are* a clever girl, Mitzi.

MITZI. Thank you, Miss Blacklock. I get you some coffee. You look tired.

MISS BLACKLOCK. That would be nice.

MITZI. Black and strong.

MISS BLACKLOCK. A little milk if you don't mind...

MITZI. Yuk! How you drink it – horrible!

*(*MITZI *exits.)*

CRADDOCK. Now, Miss Blacklock, you can relax, you're perfectly safe now.

MISS BLACKLOCK. Thank God. You might have told me you'd arranged it.

CRADDOCK. Then you wouldn't have reacted as you did. It was a little unorthodox, but it worked.

MISS BLACKLOCK. What if it hadn't?

CRADDOCK. I'd have been in a bit of a mess, wouldn't I?

MISS BLACKLOCK. What about Miss Marple?

CRADDOCK. Perhaps they've got some news down at the station. I hope to God she didn't find out about Edmund Swettenham before we did.

MISS BLACKLOCK. You'll let me know when you hear anything?

CRADDOCK. Yes. Of course.

MISS BLACKLOCK. If only she hadn't interfered...

CRADDOCK. I'll see you in the morning.

MISS BLACKLOCK. Thank you, Inspector.

*(*CRADDOCK *exits as the Main Door opens and* MITZI *enters carrying two cups of coffee.)*

MITZI. Here you are, Miss Blacklock. Nice and strong. I put just a little milk in.

(**MISS BLACKLOCK** *looks at the coffee and frowns.*)

MISS BLACKLOCK. One drop or two?

MITZI. I take a liberty. I do myself some.

MISS BLACKLOCK. Of course…

(*They sip their coffee and smile at each other. It is very insincere.*)

MITZI. Now, Miss Blacklock. We have a nice little chat.

MISS BLACKLOCK. *(warily)* Oh…

MITZI. I need money. Lots of money.

MISS BLACKLOCK. *(apparently puzzled)* Why tell me?

(**MITZI** *laughs – a small, cautious laugh.*)

MITZI. I think you will help me.

MISS BLACKLOCK. I haven't got any money, Mitzi. None to spare, that is.

MITZI. But, soon – you'll be rich. Very rich. Then you give me lots of money.

(*There is a moment's pause.*)

MISS BLACKLOCK. I, er – don't think I will…

MITZI. Oh, yes. You will. Because I help you. Now you help me.

MISS BLACKLOCK. But, I pay you to help me – with the cooking – the house…

MITZI. No, no, no. That is not what I mean. Just now, I tell a big whopper for the Inspector. Except it isn't a lie. Not this time.

MISS BLACKLOCK. You don't know what the truth is, Mitzi.

MITZI. Yes. I think I do. That policeman came to me and say, "Mitzi – you are a good liar." I say – yes, it's true! "You tell lie for me," he say. You say when you look through the keyhole you see – Miss Blacklock in the hall… "

MISS BLACKLOCK. You did your little bit very well – however, I shan't be paying you for it.

MITZI. Ah. But, he tell me to lie – and it is not a lie. For once – I tell the truth. I did see you in the hall – with a gun in your hand.

(**MISS BLACKLOCK** *stands there staring at* **MITZI**, *considering her next move.*)

You give me lots of money. I go to America to see my brother. You never hear from me again.

MISS BLACKLOCK. But you haven't got a brother, Mitzi. So, if I give you money you'll probably spend it all and then come back to see if you can get more.

MITZI. (*viciously*) I see you in the hall! You have the gun in your hand. Give me the money or I'll tell the police.

(*There is a moment's pause.*)

MISS BLACKLOCK. (*calmly*) Very well. (*She picks up the telephone.*) Here!
Phone! Phone the police. Tell them that you saw me in the hall! Tell them that you saw me with the gun. Go on! Tell them! And I'll tell them you're a liar. A liar who's trying to blackmail me.

MITZI. I'm not a liar...

MISS BLACKLOCK. And you'll be put in prison – like you say you were in your own country.

(**MISS BLACKLOCK** *thrusts the telphone in a terrified* **MITZI**'s *face and holds it there. There is a moment's pause. Clearly,* **MITZI** *is afraid.*)

I'll tell you why you won't do it. You say you were locked in the dining-room. And you *saw* me in the hall holding a gun. Well, my dishonest little Mitzi – that is another of your lies. Because the police know and everybody who was here on Friday night *knows* – that the key was in the lock. So, it was impossible for you to see anything through the keyhole!

(There is a moment's pause. **MISS BLACKLOCK** *is triumphant.* **MITZI** *is terrified.)*

Get out! Get out of here – out of my house – NOW!

*(**MITZI** exits through the Main Door.)*

*(**MISS BLACKLOCK** switches on the Dresden lamp, then closes the window curtains. The clock chimes the half-hour. She pours herself a brandy and sits. There is a moment's pause, then* **BUNNY**'*s voice is heard.)*

BUNNY'*s* **VOICE.** Lotty. Lotty. It's me, Lotty.

*(**MISS BLACKLOCK** cannot believe her ears. She rises and looks frantically around the room.)*

You're in danger, Lotty. Danger…

MISS BLACKLOCK. Bunny?

*(**MISS BLACKLOCK** is paralysed with fear. She clamps her hands over her ears but she cannot blot the voice out.)*

BUNNY'*s* **VOICE.** Lotty, Lotty.

MISS BLACKLOCK. Bunny, dear. I loved you. I really loved you. You meant so much to me. I didn't want you to die…

*(The locked door opens slightly. **MISS BLACKLOCK** gasps and moves away from it. The door swings fully open to reveal a figure standing there **MISS MARPLE** steps forward.)*

MISS MARPLE. But Bunny had to die. Everyday she was becoming more and more of a liability.

MISS BLACKLOCK. Miss Marple… Is this some kind of joke?

MISS MARPLE. I have quite a talent for mimicry, so I'm told.

MISS BLACKLOCK. A joke in the worst possible taste.

MISS MARPLE. Such sensitivity doesn't become you, Charlotte.

MISS BLACKLOCK. Charlotte is dead. I am Letitia.

MISS MARPLE. Bunny would keep referring to you as Lotty instead of Letty – at the most inconvenient times. I thought it was a slip of the tongue – I'm sure other people did, too. But she was the only one left who knew the trut – who *remembered.*

MISS BLACKLOCK. My dear woman! Bunny always muddled people's names. Everyone knew it. Mitzi for instance was often called Millie. And at times she referred to you as Miss Maple. She confused you with the London store. We were all highly amused.

MISS MARPLE. She was putting you at risk every time she got muddled. You couldn't take that risk any longer. Any moment she might give it all away.

MISS BLACKLOCK. Miss Marple. How dare you, will you please leave!

(**MISS MARPLE** *moves to the locked door as if to exit. She opens it, moves briefly outside but returns after a moment holding a Dresden lamp.*)

MISS MARPLE. Recognize it?

MISS BLACKLOCK. It's mine.

MISS MARPLE. And it used to be kept here. *(She moves to the table by the split wall and indicates the other Dresden lamp.)* But, this one replaced it. *(She holds out the length of wire attached to the lamp she is holding. We can see that it is very badly frayed.)* The flex is frayed. You can actually see the bare wire. Bunny put me on to it when she showed me the "cigarette" burn on the sideboard. She even told all of us at one point that *you* were holding the vase of violets, and *not* the cigarette-box as you insisted.

MISS BLACKLOCK. Nonsense! Another of Bunny's muddles. I was handing round the cigarettes. Phillipa will confirm it – she had one.

MISS MARPLE. All eyes were on the clock. As it finished striking you simply emptied the water on to the bare wires – that was the flash Bunny saw – and fused the lights. Very effective.

MISS BLACKLOCK. What a vivid imagination you have. I should be careful not to let it run away with you – I imagine your old age pension won't cover solicitor's fees.

MISS MARPLE. I'll risk it.

MISS BLACKLOCK. It's your funeral...

MISS MARPLE. I plan to live a few more years. When your father died. Your sister *Letitia* –

MISS BLACKLOCK. *Charlotte...*

MISS MARPLE. – decided to take you to Switzerland.

MISS BLACKLOCK. Charlotte had TB. It was the best place for her. I had the money – I loved her dearly.

MISS MARPLE. It was the right decision. You, Charlotte, *were* cured. However, ironically Letty caught pneumonia. And died. You were frantic because with her death the Goedler millions slipped through your fingers. Then it occurred to you. You and Letty had been away from England for years. There were big similarities between you. Why not swap identities with her?

MISS BLACKLOCK. My birth certificate. My passport. My bank will confirm that I am Letitia. Oh – and I even have Charlotte's death certificate.

MISS MARPLE. You came back to this country. Dora Bunner heard that Letitia had returned and contacted her because she badly needed help.

MISS BLACKLOCK. So. If I was Charlotte then Bunny would have recognized me immediately and any deception I'd planned would have been impossible.

MISS MARPLE. She did recognize you. But, when you explained to her – about Randall Goedler and the will – she actually agreed with you that it was your right to inherit the money and even offered to help you. You were lonely and here was someone who you had always had a great deal of affection for and she could substantiate your deception. You took the risk.

MISS BLACKLOCK. Good – very good.

MISS MARPLE. Everything went well for years until a few weeks ago. Then you had some bad luck. You ran into Rudi Scherz. He recognized you as Charlotte. You knew Belle could die at any moment and you knew the sort of man he was. When the news broke that you had inherited the Goedler millions, knowing that you weren't Letitia, there was a strong possibility that he would blackmail you. You dare not allow even the smallest chance of that – you'd never get rid of him.

MISS BLACKLOCK. I have my methods of dealing with blackmailers, Miss Marple.

MISS MARPLE. When Rudi Scherz came here to ask for his air fare, it was heaven sent. "Fine," you said, "next Friday is the thirteenth and I'm giving a party for my friends. I want to give them a thrill. You put an announcement in the paper saying a murder is going to take place here at six-thirty. Then turn up. I'll fuse the lights and you pretend it's a hold up. It'll scare them stiff. Then I'll give you your money."

(There is a moment's pause.)

MISS BLACKLOCK. Do go on. It's very interesting...

MISS MARPLE. You fused the lights as I explained – went through this door...

(She goes out through the locked door into the hall as she speaks.)

(Off.)... quickly along the passage, locked Mitzi in the dining-room...

(She returns through the Main Door, closing it behind her.)

... came back into the room through this door – fired two shots at yourself – except you weren't there...)

MISS BLACKLOCK. How do you account for one of the bullets nicking my ear?

MISS MARPLE. It was too obvious. *(She picks up a pair of scissors from the sofa.)* Everyone knows the ear lobe bleeds profusely when cut. A pair of scissors would do the trick. Then you shot Rudi Scherz at point-blank range. *(She puts the scissors down.)*

MISS BLACKLOCK. I'd laugh – if I didn't feel some pity for you. Feel free to tell Inspector Craddock all you've told me. He'll put it down to the rantings of a senile woman. Because we both know – there's no proof.

MISS MARPLE. Oh?

MISS BLACKLOCK. No!

MISS MARPLE. Do you remember Bunny's favourite quotation? "And sad affliction bravely borne." Switzerland is famous not only for curing TB. In a letter to you from Letitia she mentioned "iodine treatment." It baffled me for a while. But, a little research and I discovered that Swiss doctors were famous for perfecting a very special glandular operation –

(Without warning, **MISS MARPLE** *steps forward and grabs the three strings of pearls from around* **MISS BLACKLOCK***'s neck and rips them off.)*

– for goitre!

*(***MISS MARPLE***'s action reveals an ugly and vicious-looking scar which stretches right round* **MISS BLACKLOCK***'s throat.* **MISS BLACKLOCK** *screams and, during the following, backs slowly towards the scissors on the sofa.)*

I'm perfectly sure when the records are checked, we'll find out that it was Lotty and not Letty who was successfully operated on for a goitre.

*(***MISS BLACKLOCK** *looks almost insane now. She slowly advances on* **MISS MARPLE** *with the scissors behind her back.)*

What a pity you interfered. You're missing. *Presumed dead.* Edmund Swettenham stabbed you and dumped you in the river...

(**MISS MARPLE** *manoeuvres around so that* **MISS BLACKLOCK** *now has her back to the locked door.* **MISS BLACKLOCK** *advances towards* **MISS MARPLE.**)

(*Suddenly both the Main and locked Doors open.* **MELLORS** *enters through the Main Door, switches on the main lights and remains by the door.* **CRADDOCK** *enters through the locked door and, in an instant, grabs the scissors from* **MISS BLACKLOCK** *and overpowers her.*)

CRADDOCK. All right Miss Blacklock. It's all over.

MISS BLACKLOCK. (*to* **MISS MARPLE**) You interfering... There's no need to hold on to me, Inspector...

(**MELLORS** *and* **CRADDOCK** *stand on either side of* **MISS BLACKLOCK.** **MISS BLACKLOCK** *moves to the Main Door.* **MELLORS** *follows.*)

CRADDOCK. Are you all right, Miss Marple?

MISS MARPLE. Yes, thank you.

CRADDOCK. You did very well.

(**CRADDOCK** *moves through the Main Door into the kitchen, calling to the others.*)

(*Off.*) All right, everybody. Thank you very much. It's all over.

(**MRS. SWETTENHAM** *and* **EDMUND** *enter through the locked Door.*)

MRS. SWETTENHAM. You've no idea what a terrible time I've been through. I shall never forgive you – never.

EDMUND. I'm sorry, Mother. I could hardly tell you what we were up to. *You* would never have agreed to my doing it.

(**JULIA, PHILLIPA, MITZI** *and* **PATRICK** *enter through the locked door.*)

MRS. SWETTENHAM. How could you have deceived me like that?

EDMUND. I said I'd help the Inspector on the condition that I'd be the first to get all the facts. I'm convinced somewhere in all this there is a fascinating novel to be written and if I don't write it, someone else will.

JULIA. What does the Inspector want with us now?

PHILLIPA. He didn't say.

MITZI. The Inspector – tell me to come in' here and bring these. Hey – what you think of my acting – uh?

PATRICK. *(sarcastically)* Were you acting, Mitzi?

MITZI. I was even better when I pretended to blackmail Miss Blacklock. I give up cooking – and go on the stage.

(CRADDOCK enters through the locked door.)

CRADDOCK. I owe you an apology, Mrs. Swettenham. I really am sorry but the fewer the people who knew what I was up to – the better. *(To PHILLIPA.)* That's why I couldn't tell you, either.

PHILLIPA. Supposing I hadn't come to Edmund's rescue and admitted to being Pip?

CRADDOCK. There was no real danger Of that, was there? Well – now you're all here – I've got a little surprise for you. *(He moves into the hallway and fetches the chocolate cake from outside.)* I thought you'd all be in the mood to enjoy it now. Delicious Death! It's already cut – so dig in! *(He offers the cake to everyone.)*

(No one seems enthusiastic.)

Mrs. Swetenham?

MRS. SWETENHAM. No thank you. I'm on a diet.

CRADDOCK. Per-lease...

(MISS MARPLE rises from the chair and at the same time, both she and CRADDOCK take a large slice of cake each. They look at everybody else and then back to each other).

CRADDOCK. Funny people!

(With this MISS MARPLE and CRADDOCK each take a gigantic bite from their pieces of cake, as the curtain falls.)

FURNITURE AND PROPERTY LIST

ACT ONE

Scene I

Onstage:	"Craftsman's" occasional table. *On it:* Dresden shepherdess lamp, silver cigarette-box
	Sheraton bureau. *On top:* Art Nouveau china vase
	Sideboard. *On it:* tray with various drinks, including sherry, brandy, soda water; assorted glasses; flower vase
	2 small occasional tables. *On one:* telephone 6 or 7 small chairs of different styles. *On two:* newspapers
	Sofa (in window bay). *On it:* cushions
	On mantelpiece: French Empire clock
	On walls: various paintings, framed silhouettes
	Window curtains – net and velvet
	Key in Main Door
	Carpet
Offstage:	2 copies of *Chipping Cleghorn Gazette* (**PATRICK, MITZI**)
	Bunch of violets in tissue paper (**MISS MARPLE**)
Personal:	**MISS BLACKLOCK:** strings of pearls

Scene II

Strike: Newspapers

Set: Plates of sandwiches, cheesy biscuits, dip-bowl, on small centre table Loose cigarettes beside cigarette-box

Offstage: Bottle of sherry (**PATRICK**)

Flashlight (**SCHERZ**)

Revolver (**SCHERZ**)

Personal: Box of matches (**EDMUND**)

Scene III

Strike: All plates of sandwiches, etc. and dip-bowl

Violets from vase

All sherry glasses, bottles of sherry

Set: Dead violets in vase

Window curtains open

MISS MARPLE's knitting on sofa

Offstage: Torch, toy gun (**MISS MARPLE**)

Trolley with 5 cups, 5 saucers, 5 spoons, coffee-jug cream-jug, sugar-bowl, plate of biscuits (**MITZI**)

Coffee-cup (**CRADDOCK**)

Jar of honey (**MRS. SWETTENHAM**)

Personal: **CRADDOCK:** notebook, pencil, wristwatch

ACT TWO

Scene I

Strike: Toy gun and torch

Violets from vase

Trolley and coffee-cups

Set: 3 Sunday newspapers on chairs

Offstage: Wrapped package of handkerchiefs (**MISS MARPLE**)

Bag of apples (**EDMUND**)

Wrapped half-jar of honey (**MRS. SWETTENHAM**)

Bottle of aspirin (**BUNNY**)

Trolly with chocolate cake, candle in centre, cake knife, 8 small plates (**MITZI**)

Scene II

Strike:	Dirty glasses, etc.
	Newspaper
	Aspirin
	Presents
	Trolley and plates
Offstage:	Bottle of aspirin, from Scene I (**CRADDOCK**)
	Photograph album with loose letters and card (**MISS BLACKLOCK**)
	Suitcase (**MITZI**)
	2 letters, 1 sealed, 1 open (**PHILLIPA**)

Scene III

Set:	Sewing-bag with scissors readily available on sofa
Offstage:	2 cups of coffee (**MITZI**)
	Dresden shepherd lamp with frayed flex (**MISS MARPLE**)
	Chocolate cake, from ACT TWO, Scene I (**CRADDOCK**)

LIGHTING PLOT

Property fittings required: chandelier, wall brackets, 2 Dresden lamps (only 1 practical) Interior. A drawing-room. The same scene throughout

ACT ONE, Scene I. Day

To open: General effect of late autumn morning light

No cues

ACT ONE, Scene II. Evening

To open: General effect of late October afternoon light

Cue 1   **MISS BLACKLOCK** turns on main lights

             Snap on chandelier and wall brackets

Cue 2   As clock finishes chiming

             Blackout

Cue 3   **MISS BLACKLOCK:** "There's no need... " . . . . *Snap on chandelier and wall brackets*

ACT ONE, Scene III. Day

To open: As opening of ACT ONE, Scene I

No cues

ACT TWO, Scene I. Day

To open: General effect of early afternoon autumn light

No cues

ACT TWO, Scene II. Day

To open: As opening of ACT ONE, Scene I

No cues

ACT TWO, Scene III. Evening

Cue 4   As Curtain rises

             Start slow fade to dusk

Cue 5   **MISS BLACKLOCK** switches on Dresden

             lamp and closes curtains

             Snap on lamp spots; reduce overall lighting as curtains close

Cue 6   Mellors switches on main lights

             Snap on full interior lighting

EFFECTS PLOT

ACT ONE

Scene I

No cues

Scene II

Cue 1   **PHILLIPA**: "Thank you, Edmund."
                Clock chimes half-hour

Cue 2   **SCHERZ**: "Now!"
                Three revolver shots

Scene III

No cues

ACT TWO

Scene I

No cues

Scene II

No cues

Scene III

Cue 3   **MISS BLACKLOCK**: "... take a pot-shot at me." . . . *Telephone rings*

Cue 4   **MISS BLACKLOCK** closes the curtains
                Clock chimes half-hour

CPSIA information can be obtained
at www.ICGtesting.com
Printed in the USA
LVOW01s2314190916
505330LV00031B/652/P